CARDINALS *and* CROWS

Cardinals and Crows

Matthew McCarron

Charleston, SC
www.PalmettoPublishing.com

Cardinals and Crows

Hardback ISBN: 979-8-8229-0485-9
Paperback ISBN: 979-8-8229-0486-6
eBook ISBN: 979-8-8229-0487-3

These, dear reader, are excerpts from my personal journals. I am sharing them in the hopes that you may come to understand more about who I am and learn from what has been carefully curated and deemed necessary. To begin this story, I will start on a particular day in autumn. What the exact date was I don't recall; however, I was in one of the outlying villages half a mile from the city. Bishop Gregory sent me to establish a new parish in the village. It is strange to say that this instance was one of the few times I had been outside the city walls, as I was often kept close to the bishop's side or kept busy with my studies and duties. You see, dear reader, it was at the start of the previous month that the rate of disappearances had taken a sharp upturn, and Bishop Gregory had begun sending his closest confidants to encourage the peoples of our fair commonwealth to join in worship of our goddess, gain her favor, and thus be protected.

The morning this story starts was cold, and as the sun began its cresting dance across the sky, I donned my greatcoat and hat and set out for the village. For the life in the stars, I cannot remember its name. Just as well, for the village itself is not important, but as it is, the people I encountered are. My excursion took the better part of the day. The land I was greeted with outside the high walls was riddled with thick forests of oak and pine whose roots grew over every rock and stone and out of the cracks in boulders that cluttered the ground.

It wasn't until the city had sunk behind one of the land's many tree-topped, rolling hills and was out of sight that I reached into my saddlebag and removed two books of leather binding. The top was my copy of the *Church of New Light*, handed to me as a boy. It contained all the teachings of our goddess and rites and passages of the church and had been my companion for as long as my memory allowed. The bottom book, however, was what I was after. The saddlebag was small and made digging the book out on its own an impossibility. A simple-looking cover inscribed with the words *Sceldaven Runes and Rituals, by Alejandro Du Ver'.* Of all the volumes I had been able to sneak out of the bishop's libraries, his were by far the most interesting. A well-traveled man, he wrote on so much of the world outside my city walls, from the coldest, harshest tribes of the north-men to the southern tip of the continent and all the cultures and beliefs of those that inhabited them. My knuckles would be cracked with a cane for sure should Bishop Gregory learn of what I was reading. Not that it would stop me from sneaking back into the library as I had done time and time again. Through the years of tutelage, he was always kind to me and would listen to whatever question popped into my head, though he would not always answer. The sisters were far less lenient when it came to punishments for my transgressions.

The trip was rather uneventful. I occasionally looked up from the pages of my new muse to steer my horse away from the tempting branches and bushes of the roadside. I was lucky the path was large and at one point in time had been well maintained, making it easier to allow my horse to take its own reins. Most of the grass was covered by leaves and dying anyway; it escaped me what was so tempting about it. Then again, I am not a horse; therefore, I made the assumption that it was not my place to judge it for doing what a horse does.

No sooner had we rounded the corner of a tree- and bush-crowned cliff than I saw the wood wall of the village extending outward in either direction from its humble gateway. It was sooner still as I gazed forward that the wood of the wall appeared, sick. Not quite rotten, like the forlorn logs in the woods; no; this made my horse take notice as well, stopping as if hearing a predator lurking nearby but never taking her eyes away from the wooden structure. A faint yellow hue encapsulated the air around us, and the lack of noise from inside was deafening. The silence was broken only by one lone pikeman sitting on the ground and tossing pebbles into the small, diminished fire that kept him company.

As I approached the gate, I did my best to shake my nerves away and addressed the guard. "Hello, good sir. My name is Jaccob Myers; I'm a priest of the Church of New Light. I'm here on behalf of the bishop." He looked up at me in a time of his own making. His eyes had sunken in and were adorned in the dark rings brought by exhaustion. He looked me up and down in that same tired, self-crafted pace as before and answered "Gate's open" before returning to his fire.

After dismounting, I indeed found the gate opened with the smallest of resistance. The lack of sound was prevalent, and this sent a chill through me, as I could clearly see a handful of townsfolk carrying out their daily chores, trudging through the muddied streets and square, their eyes fashioned with the same dark rings of exhaustion. From what I was told, I was to expect the village mayor to greet me. Instead, no one cared to pay me any mind. In fact, I seemed to be in the way as people lazily brushed past. There was an inn close to the entrance, so I made my way to its stable to hitch my horse. The inside was simple and warm, with wooden furnishings and a fire. The keeper, a woman with a firm scowl, waited for me to address her. "Hello, ma'am, I am Jaccob Myers. I was sent by Bishop Gregory," I said to her.

"Hats off inside," she replied. Not angry or annoyed even at the fact I had forgotten my manners. Just tired. I removed my hat and apologized, and she looked in the ledger on the counter she stood behind. "Middle initial." She beckoned.

"*M*," I replied, "Jaccob M. Myers."

She continued, "Church has paid for two days' stay. Room is up the stairs, second door on the left, bath through the door to my right. Food and drink in the tavern—that's in the square—mayor's commission across the street from that, and the morgue is on the south end." She placed a key on the counter and exited through a door behind her and locked it. Her exit was so abrupt I had no time to ask why I needed to know where the morgue was. Taking the key, I spied the ledger on the counter. It had only two names written on the visible pages, my own and some scrawled lettering I couldn't make out, dated some months prior.

I quickly placed my few belongings inside the room and my books on the small desk next to the window. Afterward I made my way back down the stairs, out the door, and toward the village square. It was a short walk to the mayor's commission. Odd it was, I thought, as I walked through the mud and noticed large planks of wood stacked in front of the buildings and homes, some with nails sticking out at the ends. I knocked on the door to the mayor's building and waited. The door creaked slowly open, revealing a small man advanced in years. He let out a gasp of realization as he recognized my affiliation and led me inside. There was a large uncomfortable moment of silence between us. The man certainly wasn't what I had been expecting.

After clearing my throat, I broke the strained, dark silence with "Mayor—"

"She's at the morgue," he interrupted.

"I beg your pardon?" I asked.

"That's why you're here, isn't it?" he asked. He must have seen my confusion, for he sighed and beckoned me to follow him out the door. He led me through the mud streets of the village, which began to narrow the farther in we went among the old wooden buildings. The wood looked as though it should have been taken by rot but refused to give. The alleyways revealed a smell I had been privy to but was not wholly aware of when I entered. There was a mixture of mud and dirt, of course, lined with the lazy disposal of feces, and there was an underlying smell of decay. It would have been explained away by that same lazy disposal if I wasn't disturbed at the smell so much that my eyes were drawn to the ground neath my feet as if the smell was seeping up from under the soil or from the soil itself. By my observations the ground almost seemed the same yellow that hung in the air and clung to the walls. I asked the man why sanitation laws were being ignored.

He replied, "Scared. People are too scared to travel outside the gates to the stream." He went on to explain how even the latrine in the mayor's office had overflowed and how he had no inclination of going outside the gates.

I was disgusted by the information he gave and thought how lucky we both were. One, that I would be greeted with the shit and piss of all those who lived here and two, that on my return to the city, I would report this infraction to the duke. A town so rife with filth would surely breed disease. Finally, we rounded the way to the gates of the moss-covered stone building. It was now I smelled the heavy aroma of a process I was unfamiliar with.

Mayor Sevil Armre' El made her introduction as the door to the closeted morgue shrieked open. There the mayor lay on a tall stone slab, eyes wide, mouth agape. The mortician tended to what was left of what could be identified as a torso only from the presence of a head. The only sound brave enough to escape me was the noise of my boots scraping the floor as I recoiled in shock.

"We pulled her from the ground in her office," said my guide. "She was stuck half in the floorboards by the time we forced the door open. Bless the body now, for these will be the last eyes to see her before she is placed below."

Admittedly I was too much in shock to give a reply, be it verbal response or meeting their eyes, and so I stood, anchored to the stone, fighting to regain my composure. "I am to understand she was not a member of the church?" The words poured out of me like sludge from a clogged pipe.

"That is the reason you are here, I had reckoned. To bring our village into the light of the church? Bless our grounds and offer salvation?" the man pried.

"I'll need my book and some water," I replied. Quickly I turned away to escape the lifeless screaming eyes of the late mayor, and so I trudged my way, confused and sickened, back to the inn. The image of Sevil Armre' El would not shake free from my mind: eyes rolled back into the skull seeming to call out, begging for help even with a lack of pupils. I made my way up the stairs and into my room. I grabbed my effects off the desk and stopped just a moment to look out my window. Then I noticed my window had no shutters to close at night. I placed my books back down and hung my head out the portal with some caution, turning my gaze to the sill and outer walls. A wasp crawling out of a hole gave me the answer I did not realize I was looking for. Above the little creature's exit and below it were more holes of strikingly comparable size and a patterned width apart. Nail holes. Hanging from my window, I peered into the ongoings of the folk below steadily delivering their stacks of wood planks and bars into their homes. For the moment I chose to ignore this puzzling action.

Once returned to the morgue, I carried out my responsibilities as a priest. The proper passages read; the remains consecrated with holy water and all the while I was numb to the ever-closing walls around me. I barely heard my own words and was brought back to the foreground of consciousness by the smell of the mortician's chemicals infusing itself inside the rotting aroma of the village.

Next was the village itself. One of the townsfolk had a garden where a bush of thistle was battling against the autumn air. With her permission, I gathered a branch to dip into a bucket of blessed water. Fastening the stalks of thistle into a wand, I commanded every mud-dressed alleyway, every nail-ridden door and window, and even the village gate to be a shield of the Goddess Erëdna herself so that these people might be brought into the church and saved from their plight.

A small congregation of folk had followed me to the gate and watched as I sprinkled water with thistle and bucket. I saw no hope in their eyes, no relief. They simply stood, watched, and followed. They followed me all around the village until I stepped outside the gates to finish my holy walk. It was a silent moment before their backs were shown to me and they returned to repurposing the planks outside their homes. Nails and all the strips of wood were lugged past the entryways into what should have been their havens.

Walking past an open window on my way to retirement at the inn, I spied the new use of the nails and wood. The gentleman I saw nailed the planks onto the existing floorboards. He stopped and met my eyes with his own. Not a word was spoken between us, but he spoke volumes with his eyes. Understandably so, his face twisted into an expression of discomfort at being watched from his open window, and then he reached beside him to retrieve a second hammer. He held the handle outstretched to me. I entered, removed my coat and hat, and knelt beside the man. We hammered the nails into place and adjusted the planks as needed. Any space left for furnishings was only a second thought in the man's mind, and to that end the few furnishings he had were used in the spaces a plank would not do. Not a word was spoken. The air was too heavy to allow that.

Sunlight was shining near parallel to the ground by the time I closed the door to my rented room. I had not eaten, nor had I washed away the smell from my travels. I was on the second floor, and the sun was fading, so I decided I'd eat and bathe in the morning's light. Despite much of my body petitioning for a rest, I decided against that. My breathing was heavy, yet I did everything I could to stifle that sound out of chilling fear I had no sway over. I was on the second floor, and that was good. I knew it was good. I latched my door and dragged the single dresser the room provided in front of it. My lamp burned bright, and I fed it at the slightest dimming. My thoughts thrashed about my skull like a hurricane unleashing its power upon an unprepared coast. Droplets of sweat formed on my brow as I squirmed in my chair trying to find even the smallest semblance of comfort. Calm is what I needed now. I took my book in hand—the simple covered one I kept hidden in my satchel—and opened to the chapter entitled "A Connection of Mind and World." The pages offered a plethora of knowledge proposing questions and vague wordy answers that required my undivided attention to understand. For a time, I was lost within its pages; however, I was unable to keep the distraction.

My attention was soon given to my open window. The sun had sunk, and the moon offered no refuge from the thickening darkness that mimicked the mud of the streets below. It wrapped around every corner and hid the world from view just as if my eyes had been shut. I would have thought they were if not for my lantern fighting to keep the night from crawling into my room. I sat for what might have been hours or could have been mere minutes, eyes and ears fixed on the small square opening between me and the lack of world outside it. I could smell it. All at once I could smell it as if it were in the very room lurking behind me. That horrid odor of rot dug into the air and set every hair on end. It was moving.

Just as quickly as it grew, the smell faded to a new corner of the darkness without releasing its grip on the air. The air itself being choked by the stench was greeted with a second sensation. A growing, howling sensation.

I dropped my book and fell back from my chair, never removing my eyes from the darkness. I was cold. I was cold and frozen at the sound of a man screaming gutturally, from the lowest depths of his lungs. The helpless, damning scream of a wounded animal followed by the concussion of black powder. Two more shots in succession, this time the muzzle flashes being seen straight out from my window silhouetting the structures that separated us shrouded in a thick yellow haze.

More shouting came from the direction of the mayor's office. The streets lit up with the lanterns of those running toward the shrill plea for help, muskets and pistols in hand. The shouting continued and emanated from where smoke now hung above the roofs, illuminated by the lanterns below. Women and men barking orders; then suddenly, silence. The smell had moved once more and vanished.

I don't know how long I stood frozen with my eyes fixed on the black. I trembled out the word "fuck" and removed the dresser from the door, threw my coat and hat on, snatched up my lantern, and grasped the handle of the door. I stood frozen again as I tried to will myself to remove the latch. The hall was empty. Still silence rang. The stairs descending to the first floor cracked and moaned. Silence again.

Holding my lantern so, I followed the fresh, frantic boot prints in the mud until the light of it met with the light of the others. The pikeman from the gate sat slumped with his head in hand and his back to a house. Those I had seen running had gathered inside. The door was intact. The windows intact. My eyes fell to the same spot the ragtag militia had so diligently been watching. The floorboards had been broken and lying across the gaping maw of the dank earth below was a musket still grasped by a white-knuckled severed hand, its remaining blood feeding into the hole beneath it.

People began to shuffle out the vacant building, some stifling sobs into sniffles and barely lifting their eyes past the ground. The fingers were loosened from the weapon, and the hand was tossed down the hole, the rifle collected. The person I assumed to be the leader of the militia stared at me through welling eyes. What was I to say? All manner of text and scripture ran through my head in response to the scene I had witnessed, all vying for a chance to console someone. But what was I to say?

"Help me cover the hole." She choked back tears.

A sturdy table was laid across it first, then a wooden bed frame. We both struggled to move these items together, which was a small relief to me. She then stood in the doorframe and hesitated before stepping out into the street.

I joined the ambling survivors in the short trudges back to their homes. Where some turned to the tavern, I made my way back to the inn, though after placing my hands on the door, I couldn't help but consider downing a pint. I stepped inside to meet the innkeeper behind the counter once more. She was scratching in a page of the book where my name was written. "Oh, I heard your steps out the door and assumed you'd left for good what with all the commotion, sir." She dropped the quill back into its pot and turned to exit.

"What was that?" I called out.

"It's what you was sent for, wasn't it?" she replied.

I explained to her that I was sent to bring the town into the light of the church, that there was an unsanctioned pagan community, and I was to speak to the mayor about building a parish here. I continued, saying there hadn't been horrors in Târgaiova for nearly fifty years, let alone an attack so close to the city.

"When's the last you traveled out the city?" She looked me over with an almost disgusted expression. "I've been hearing of attacks since I was a young lady. And these ones, the one you saw tonight, have become frequent."

I interjected, "How so?"

She continued, "More and more of the outlying villages are reporting attacks. All of the same manner too. Where one village might be quiet for a night, another will lose people to the ground. Always at night." She corrected herself, "Usually at night."

I proceeded to ask why aid had not been sent in the form of soldiers and healers or wagons to relocate the people back to the city. The now-exasperated innkeeper said I was the aid. A dispatch had been sent, and I had arrived in reply. Blessing the grounds was supposed to drive off the creatures that made the darkness their home. The innkeeper then turned and closed the door behind her, leaving me in the foyer with naught but lamplight and questions.

There had to be something I could do. There was something I could do. I was a priest of Erëdna, and by her light I would see these monsters stopped. I'd rest what little I could for the night, and in the morning, I would speak to the town. There had to be someone who knew more and could lead me to answers. Amazingly, I found darkness behind my eyes if not for the body exhausting itself. Morning came, and by the first rays of light, my fist met the door of the mayor's office.

"No one's in there." The voice of the old man came accompanied by the small rattling of a key ring. "Couldn't sleep either, I suppose?" he pushed out with heavy breath. He fumbled with the lock to the office foyer and pushed the door in and waved me inside.

"I've been terribly rude, sir. I never caught your name," I said as I kept the door from swinging back, however gentle it would have been.

The man's eyes snapped up to mine with the light of a face remembering an old, happy memory. He introduced himself as Lonut, Michiheal Lonut. Both smiling faintly, indulging in the pleasantry, we introduced ourselves until Lonut shifted his weight from one side to the other and asked the purpose of my visit. His posture sank when I revealed I'd come to ask questions about the night. He took a moment to himself before mentioning that coffee and breakfast would be needed. Patiently I sat and waited in the foyer of the office, looking at the portraits of those that had served behind these doors. The locked door to the mayor's desk room caught my attention, particularly the series of locks and a humble yet hastily made pull bar lying across it.

A tray of coffee and buttered bread in hand, Lonut reemerged. "That was the third night. One night before you arrived." He placed the tray down on a small table and had me help remove the bar to the door. After the locks were opened, I could see the mess the room had been thrust into. He explained the scene to me. He offered information on how Mayor Armre' El had stayed late to write after the second attack. A few of the villagers had gone missing, he continued, including a few children, a farmer, and a gate guard. He told me the farmer had gone missing during daylight and all that was found were scratch marks and tattered, bloodied clothes hanging on a fence post. It wasn't until the night of the mayor's death, when they found the mayor sticking half out of the floor, that they learned it came from the earth beneath their feet.

"What was she writing? Why did the mayor stay late?" I asked.

"Letters. Two of them. She wrote one to the church and one to the Order of Crows."

Every muscle in my body tightened, and my breath grew short at the mention of the order.

"I believe she was on her way out to send them before…" he stuttered out. "We all heard her scream. Gods, I still hear her. I was too slow to reach her in time with the others. The letters were finished, so I sent them the same night. Two riders." His eyes began to water, and his breath caught in his throat. Sobbing, he fell to the floor; I ran to catch him, bring him back to his feet. All I could do was place my hands on his shoulders, muttering, "My friend, I'm so sorry."

I helped him to his chair, and silently we finished our coffee and bread together. Lonut seemed to be thankful for this, though he hardly made a sound. After some time, he expressed his need to be alone; he had to address the possibility of abandoning the town and distributing the remaining revenue accordingly, so I thanked him and left.

Standing in the square, I thought as to what I should do next. I could ride back to the bishop and listen to his counsel. He would know how to comfort my mind and direct me where I needed. But no—no, I couldn't abandon these people; the ride would take too long on its own. There must have been a reason the consecration of the grounds didn't work.

I looked across the town at the ambling people until my eyes came to the tavern. The room was empty; all the tables and chairs and even the barstools, the legs of which had been cut off and fashioned into stakes, had been stripped and nailed down to the floor. From behind the bar emerged a scrawny man in an apron who, upon seeing me, quickly exclaimed, "We ain't open." Calmly I told him that I came just to ask the location of someone. He spat at me, "Why don't you ask the location from your goddess? Why don't you ask why you and your damn church ain't done shite to help us? We don't want you here."

I continued speaking. "The woman who led last night's militia, I wish to speak with her."

The man's eyes squinted, and he drew short breaths, taking all the time he could to think about the words. "South side. Follow the trail to the farm. Ain't far. Now git." I tipped my hat, thanked the man, and promptly turned to leave. As the door was closing behind me, I heard the scrawny barkeep mumble to himself, "Fuckface."

The distance was short indeed and covered by a thicket of trees skirted with large rocks. At the path's end lay a disheveled cow pen attached to a humble, similarly disheveled home. There was a cart with various items placed carefully on top of one another. Inside, with the look of stone, the woman I had sought out stood in the portal. Mara, she introduced herself, and expressed a concern for the passage of time as I had caught her in the middle of packing her things. She was so concerned that I was given only the amount of time it took for her to finish wrapping a few belongings and parcels of food to speak my mind. "You were not sent at the request of the letter?" Thankfully, she sat down.

I explained that I had been sent to bring the village into the fold. There was a quick sneer that flashed across Mara's face but quickly faded away. Mara and I talked across from each other for what must have been an hour until we came to a conclusion. I had come looking for answers and caught her as she was preparing to leave for the city. She had swayed a few more, mostly those that had followed her into the thundering darkness of the night before, to abandon their homes and depart for the city with her. She was not able to provide more information on the attacks other than that of the death of her husband, pulled down into the dirt, surrounded by squealing, panicking cows.

Thus, we came to our conclusion. The letter—or, more precisely, the courier—had never made it to the steps of Cathedral Gregori. She suggested that I might be able to understand more if I could determine the location and circumstances of the missing messenger. There was only the one road in between the gate of the town and the gates of the city; with the combined eyes of the night's militia and myself, we might be able to find a clue. So, I agreed; at the least I might be able to accomplish something. My belongings in hand, I met my companions at the foot of the inn, and we set off, eyes peering at the edges of a beaten path and wild uncertainty.

Groans and sighs filled the air, and each member of our downtrodden party took quick glances over a shoulder. Each person would turn for different reasons, I was sure; some longed to see the return of the hope that once was their home, to feel the warmth of their hearth on a cold night and hear the laughter of a neighbor through an open window. Some glanced back to find another walking at a pace slower than wanted or expected and would wait to join them at their side. For Mara and me, the reasons were that and more. She and I spoke very little the time we walked together. The sounds were naught but the snapping of twigs and the rolling of pebbles in the path. My horse was pulling a wagon of various belongings and supplies; the winding, narrow road framed by dense woods and steep cliffs made the journey that much slower with wagon and heavy heart in tow.

Night would fall before we made it to the walls of the city. A camp would have to be made. I had never made camp before, and I might have been excited to do so in any other circumstance, but frustration, hunger, and the aching of my legs kept any notion of novelty from my mind. There was little in the way of open space in which to set up tents and fires, as the road itself was wide but shadowed by large rock formations on one side and a cliff on the other. We made do with the space on the road itself, tying off tents to trees and stringing them across to another. Some openings in the face of the rock walls allowed for small wood frames to be lodged and various necessities to be strewn across. Before the sun had crawled its way out of sight, in the reds and pinks that marked the end to comfortable visibility, we transformed the road into what could easily have been a working community. The lights of fires bouncing off faces were charming. Nothing could be heard, though, but the crackling of those fires. We all held our breath.

One by one my weary companions began closing their eyes and wrapping themselves in blankets and coats, holding each other as they embraced sleep. I was not so lucky. One of my hands began to shake, my eyes darted at the slightest rustle of the leaves in the wind, and the wind grew stronger as the night grew older. I breathed in deep, hoping not to recognize that odor of the plagued streets and homes of the small degrading village.

Mara, after diligently walking from end to end of the camp and digging a trench in the dirt, finally came to rest at my fire, offered a cup of steaming coffee, and sat down across from me. For some time, we sat in silence, leering over the small flickering flames. We broke into stilted conversation, discussing the missing rider. What were the contents of the letter? Why was there no trace of the rider? I thought that perhaps we had missed something. There were plenty of distractions, with the noise of the caravan and the events of the night past squeezing their icy fingers around my thoughts ever tighter. Mara suggested that with the path ahead, there might yet be a chance at finding a clue. This road was the only one between Mara's village and my city. Any path leading to a destination elsewhere lay in the city itself or on its far side. Assuming that our messenger was still alive, we guessed at possible destinations he might have taken and the reasons for such decisions.

We spoke at length, with our conversation succeeding in answering not a single question. "Perhaps there are too many of us," I said. "Too many in one place. Or maybe we've traveled far enough outside its hunting grounds."

Mara side-eyed me before retrieving her musket. I watched as she cleaned it, meticulously checking every rivet, every inch, from butt to barrel tip. She rolled her sleeves to her elbows and wrapped around her forearm was a tattoo. While I didn't immediately understand it, I was able to piece it together. From my time spent sneaking into the library and stealing books, I semi recognized several tribes' runes inscribed around an intricate knotted band. The runes were a mixture of those of the northern Sceldaven tribes and their neighboring Highlands. The meanings gathered were that a few chosen deities had been asked to bless the bond of two who had shared a lifetime together. A marriage not of doe-eyed strangers or political bindings but of two full lives choosing to walk into twilight with one another.

I struggled with the thought of asking her to explain the runes and knots I did not understand, but believing it to be for the better, refrained from doing so. My time reading certainly helped in my silent understanding, however. Runes are not words per se, as you are reading now. They are contextual abstractions and ideas that, when written together, may have a great multitude of meanings. I was able to derive the notion of guidance and favor from the images of her gods and magics but most notably discerned that her band was meant to represent a life bond with what I assumed was now her late husband. Those of the northern tribes didn't marry in the same sense that those of the church did. Directly speaking, I didn't understand the practice.

I looked away and focused on not spilling my coffee with my hands shaking so; uncontrollably my thoughts jumped from one to another without finishing until eventually I formed the words: "I'm going to go back. At first light I'm going to travel back to the village." Mara looked at me inquisitively but said nothing. "There's a chance we missed something, and I may be able to find it on the way back, and you might continue looking on the way forward. There are still many who chose to stay in the village, and I cannot leave them."

She looked through me with an expression harder than stone. "Have you ever used a musket before?" she inquired. I shook my head. The rest of the windy, sleepless night, she took great care in showing me the proper way to hold, load, and fire the musket and had me repeat everything back to her. When sufficiently satisfied, she showed me the proper care for the powder and bearings.

Light broke over the treetops, and so it was that fires were doused and tents were struck. Mara, with a noticeable glint of hope in her eye, clasped my hand in hers and shook before moving the caravan forward. I let them keep the horse. I'll admit I wish I could have seen myself weighted with a sack of books and belongings, musket slung over my shoulder and a pouch each for powder and bearings, but all notion of novelty was again far from my mind. It would take me some time to arrive at the gates once more with the newfound burdens that I was not particularly ready for. With every footfall forward, I grew cold, and my hands continued to shake, with my breath following. I wish I could say I spent my time navigating the possibilities of what lay before me; however, I could think of nothing but my ever-shaking body and the cold sweat running down my brow. To keep myself occupied, it was all I could do to look out at the rays of light shining through branches and over stone and dancing past the brim of my hat. I focused on this and trying to steady my breathing. This self-appointed task proved time consuming enough.

Finally I came to that sickly, yellowed haze hanging in the air, clinging to an ever-ailing, rotten set of gates. Or more accurately, a gate. Much of the wooden wall that had greeted me at my first entrance was missing, leaving but an indention in the ground where it had once stood. My question as to where it all could have gone was quickly answered by the constant sound of hammering and sawing and the distant shouting of commands. I glanced up at the inn and silhouetted by the light was the now-grotesque facade. Where was once a charming inn with simple walls and pointed roofing now stood a hastily built fort of repurposed wood, iron, and rope. Narrow walkways, landings, and manned watchtowers were now a fixture of the sky above me. Makeshift bridges extended out to the roofs of adjoining homes.

"It's the priest!" was shouted out from somewhere in the bones of the wooden creature swallowing the inn before me. No sooner had I spotted the watchman than the door leading inward was flung open, and a quick ushering beckoned me inside the belly of this mangled beast. Little time was given for me to take in the surroundings of the once-familiar foyer, now storage room. The stairs, too, moved almost by themselves beneath me; the lodgings packed with people, tools, and keepsakes rushed by. I was led to a single small attic room where a hole had been cut to serve as the portal to the outside landing.

Here I could see down into the homes whose walls had been stripped and those currently undergoing the renovations. The foundations and support beams had been left to be used as stilts. The wind was unkind, and the smell of the streets wafted higher than our refuge, leaving an unpleasant watering in the eyes. There had been no time to cover the platforms with roofing, so in place were old sheets and rags strewn over tolerable bedding.

A familiar voice quaked from behind me. I turned to see Lonut shambling out of the attic. We both had a sigh of relief at the sight of one another. We embraced, and a flurry of questions erupted from both of us. Lonut asked about Mara and if we had been attacked on the road; I explained that no harm had come our way and that they should have reached the city safely. I asked if there had been another attack. There had been. Three people were taken whole, dragged under the ground. It would have been more had the creatures not refused to step out of the homes they had dug into. The remaining villagers had worked through the night to build the shelter with help from refugees from another village. Then Lonut explained the long process they had taken to achieve this architectural wonder together. There were those that took shifts as watchmen who would be relieved of said duty only to relieve those tasked with construction, and those on construction would be relieved for rest. Those that were resting would be woken for watch duty and so on.

Lonut, needing to leave the conversation due to the strain of his age, asked about the letter—if we had found the rider sent to deliver it and if Mara was safe. He grew quiet, doing his best to hide his worries. Another helped him back inside.

There I stood, looking around at the people huddled over the quaintest of fires and under would-be tents. Some of their eyes met mine with anticipation as others met with indifference, and some clearly would rather I not be there at all. There was an open space on one of the smaller platforms across from the inn. I made my way across the rickety bridge held together by a miracle and settled into the space, placing my personal belongings onto a bedroll. Keeping Mara's gifts with me, I began asking to speak with the night's survivors. It was incredibly easy deriving information, although many of the witnesses had questionably different stories as to the events that had occurred, and some spoke incoherently with a fresh fear dripping from their eyes and loss crushing down on their hearts. In their stories of the earth opening and claims of spirits emerging from the depths of darkness, I noticed two similarities. First, the attacks had taken place in the homes—specifically the homes that were being deconstructed. Second, each person described the overwhelming smell of death just before a new hole would be pierced in the ground.

The sun was beginning to set, and I had been volunteered for watch. The wind was a cool, relentless kiss upon my cheeks; fortunately, my bolero shielded my eyes from the drizzle of colder rain falling from the darkening blanket that selfishly grasped the shine of the moon and stars. I sat in reflection on the events of the past days, trying to make any connection that might lead me to understand them. I came to the conclusion that I was entirely in over my head. It was at this point, with the rain drizzling off the brim over my eyes, that the barkeep approached and as politely as possible offered me a mug and a small, fresh pot of coffee. I didn't notice the shakes in my hand again until I had to focus on not spilling said coffee.

I refused the rotating change in watch, for I could not bring the idea of sleep into a comfortable space in my mind. Instead, I acquainted myself with the thick, miasma-like smell of death and decay and the scent that seemed so familiar in the recesses of my mind. The phantom, hidden from my eyes, came and went all through the night at intervals that were erratic. The direction was always difficult to determine, as it seemed to change at will.

Halfway through pouring what must have been my fifth coffee, I was struck by the overwhelming smell I had tried to become accustomed to. My throat clenched and retched; my stomach begged to remove its contents. I was inclined to agree with it. That was before I heard the scratching. It was like the sound of fingernails carelessly scraping against half-rotten wood followed by the undeniable snapping of the floorboards beneath my landing. I froze, hoping my body wouldn't betray me with sounds of disgust. The scraping slid its way to where the door would have been.

As carefully and quietly as I could, I grabbed my lantern in one hand, the rail in the other, and I leaned myself over. I could see so little through the dark and the rain, and my lantern's light only glittered back at me off the drops in the air. Hesitating, I lowered my lantern, and there it was. A hand so large I could make the details out from my position so high—so dark and cloaked a hand, emaciated, held together by nothing more than rotten muscle tissue and cartilage wrapped in a shining muck—and it was oddly concave. The palm must have been bulged outward to the back of the hand, and the fingers were long, consisting of more joints than I dared take the time to count. The hand reached out of the frame toward the street, and I could see that the shining muck was not that at all but its flesh, tighter than a corpse's skin and paler still.

At the instant the hand made contact with mud street, a hollow crackle came from under the bones with the sharpest, quickest flash of blue flames and a piercing screech! A scream that was a combination of ghastly gurgles! The hand pulled back quick enough to smother the bright-blue burning flames. I heard my own voice echoing the creature's horrible, blasphemous one only after the scraping and snapping slipped back into the hole it must have crawled out of. I looked around at the other watchman on guard, all staring at me or the bones of the home I sat upon.

Another scream came from the adjacent platform; this time the voice was distinctly human. As quickly as it had disappeared into the dark, the creature arose from the depths of the mud underneath her platform. The scream came from the realization that the support beams were being ripped apart. The immediate shift in weight broke the bridge free, sending it crashing to the ground. The watchman held on to the skyward rail as another beam snapped with what seemed to be the faintest of effort. I don't know what came over me or if it even was me, but in the blink of an eye I was halfway across my own bridge, musket in hand. I hardly felt the floor as I moved faster than I ever had before. I leaped over huddled couples and skipped down the stairs. One person opened the door and stepped out of the way in time for me to fling myself outward. The platform then folded in on itself and blanketed the guard in splintered boards and rusty nails.

She was still alive as she was buried, her lantern swinging on a hook still attached above. She was still alive as the creature began digging its way to her. With a flick of its wrist, wood and nail were torn from their rest and lived in the air! My legs stopped at the threshold, and musket met shoulder. At the sound of the hammer cocking, the creature turned to me and met my eyes. I saw its own by the swinging, mocking light of the swaying lantern above. Lidless, cold, deformed, and shining like the eyes of a coyote. They were all I could see before my hand squeezed. My shoulder caught the butt, and the air was pushed from my lungs as I landed on the flat of my back!

I could hear it snap the last of the barricade between it and the guard. Her calls for help were cut short by gasps and then silence. Gnashing my teeth and bearing the weight of an airless body, I dug both hands into the mud, and with every bit of breath my lungs could grasp, I threw myself to my knees and hurled the mud in my hands toward the hulking shadow. A flash of blue flames wrapped around howling, screeching horror! It fled back down into the dark of the ground flames, stench and howling disappearing down with it.

More of the townspeople rushed by me to aid the guard. She was hurt, bleeding from where a leg should have been. One person began shoveling mud down into the hole while others rushed to the woman's aid and carried her to a room inside the inn. While some townspeople spent the rest of the night shoveling mud into each hole in each home close to the inn, I chose to help those caring for my fellow watchman and tending to her wounds. She passed in her sleep. I awoke slumped against the wall the next morning, jostled to consciousness by the hurried tones of alerted voices carrying through the halls.

I followed them down the stairs and out the door into the street. Standing inside the wreckage were Lonut and a woman I did not recognize. She was crouched near a still-standing beam on the inside of the bones. With little effort she pulled from it what looked to be a bullet lodged into the wood. After I had fired, the bullet must just have bounced off the body of the creature and had stuck itself in. After pulling it out, she stood.

The woman was six feet tall, broad shouldered, and had the darkest skin, like the night sky. She was clad in chain mail and a brigandine adorned with three belts holding various pouches and bags, and I saw at least three one-handed weapons strapped to her body, with more of all aforementioned on a bag slung across her back. The most impressive part was that nothing was out of place. The armor was worn in such a way that made her movements seem like those of a bird gliding through the air, and each pouch, bag, and belt was carefully placed to be accessible without hindrance. A black cloak draped across her shoulders with gray and red highlights caught the eye and my memory. The woman turned to look at me. Pinned on and holding her cloak in place was the image of an eastern red-tailed crow.

She spoke neither harshly nor calmly, but plainly. She asked nothing more than what she wanted to know and said nothing more than what was required. Georgetta Oana, she introduced herself as and inquired about my involvement in the matters of the village, how long I had been here, what I had seen and heard. She was patient with me and accepted the coffee I offered as I tried not to spill it. There was a small flicker in her eyes as I talked about my blessing of the streets, the use of the mud to drive away the creature, and she bore a surprised expression upon learning I had chosen to return to the village after leaving. She sat silent, presumably to take in the information I had given her, before urging me to lead her to the morgue. So I did.

We trudged through the mud and muck to where I was greeted with the horrified visage of the mayor. As Georgetta and I rounded a corner to bring the small moss-covered building into view, she stopped me dead in my tracks with a single arm across my chest. We both stared at each other quietly before agreeing in the same silence that there was a scratching sound coming from inside the house next to us—the same snapping of wood and dragging of ragged claws that had pierced through the clatter of falling rain the night prior. This, however, was less intrusive. The home was too far to have been elected for restructure, and its roof had a noticeable round in it that matched no other building.

Georgetta's eyes fixed first; following her line of sight to the window, behind the glass, I saw two deformed, glinting eyes that sank into the darkness of the home. She entered first and drew out a short sword. Its blade was lined with what looked to be silver around the tip and edges. It was not an elegant lining containing patterns throughout but a simple dripping of silver onto an already existing blade. This is not to suggest that it was crude or uneven; it was done with purpose of practicality. The air was still and ripe with the smell of corpse and decay; I followed behind Georgetta; the only sounds to be heard were our footfalls and the incessant thudding of my heart pounding in my ears.

The home was quaint, single roomed with small alcoves in a few of the walls. There was an all-too-familiar-looking hole in the floorboards on the far side, large and muddied. Furniture was tossed around, dusty and highlighted by the cracks in the ceiling. In those same bowed-out cracks, I could see blood, dried from time, and a small stretch of fabric torn from the tunic of what must have been the former owner.

Georgetta turned to me. "It would seem your monster ran into a short fight with this one. Threw the victim into the ceiling to end it." She knelt down. "The table was used to cover the hole and was then thrown aside." She pointed to the hilt of a cooking knife lying on the floor. The blade was broken and lay some steps away. "Whoever fought gave the others a chance to escape."

Small as it was, the home was meant for more than one; I hadn't wanted to admit it to myself on entry. But the thought of others escaping was a small comfort.

Georgetta continued her observation of our confined surroundings, wearing an expression that to me suggested she was largely unsatisfied by what she could see. There was a gurgle, deep and guttural, emanating from the wall the hole occupied. My hairs stood on end, my skin felt frozen, and in that moment a grotesque, gnarled hand reached out from behind Georgetta and wrapped its bone fingers around her leg! I hardly saw it. She spun around like the crack of a whip, twisting her sword wrist to slash the blade up into the arm. The sword caught and stuck in the forearm of the creature, a steady smoke and sizzling rising from the very same. Georgetta's hand slipped from the blade.

In the midst of an unearthly howl, the creature pulled back into its hole, sword still stuck into its now-burning arm. Georgetta reached down after it and grasped the creature around its head, deadlifting it out of its hole. All the skin of our shrieking, writhing abomination burst into the same smoke with each contact of the armor she wore as she wrestled the beast to ground and pinned it. It was strong. Almost too strong; Georgetta was losing her grip as she shouted to me, "Neck! Stab it!"

I rushed in, yanked the blade from the arm, and plunged the silver and steel into its neck. The skin of the creature was taut and tough. I dropped the sword in the neck of the beast again and again and again, smoke and burning flesh wrenching from the wounds, until finally I removed its disgusting head from its shoulders. Its body, its proportions, were wrong. Emaciated to a point where I could see organs under its skin, hands too large for its arms, a head bulbous and caved in, and a stomach, a stomach that was obviously well fed.

Georgetta sneered at it. "Take me to the morgue," she said.

"What is this filth?" I asked.

She grasped my shoulder and pushed me out the door. "Now," she said.

The morgue was cold and dark and smelled of chemicals. On the far side of the center table was a door leading to a descending staircase. Georgetta silently took in the surroundings and very carefully analyzed each and every bottle, vial, and container of chemicals and tools. She looked for cracks, stains, and inconsistencies in the labels and placements. She put each item back in place on its shelf and closed the cabinet doors. She turned to the far door of the small room, opened it, and looked me in the eye. I took my wand, dipped it in water, and sprinkled the walls and stairs with the intent that each drop would reach as far as possible down into the dark.

Georgetta stood on top of the island table to reach a candlelight lantern. I observed as she opened the casing to the lantern, held her hand close to the wick, and focused. For a moment all was still until suddenly the wick began to shimmer with a small flame growing into existence. She closed the casing, and we proceeded down the stairs. The landing was small, too, housing only a few coffins of previous mayors and two wealthy landowners from the village.

"I'm correct in understanding this village does not belong to the church?" Georgetta asked over her shoulder.

I answered yes.

She continued, telling me not to use the water and to leave the searching of the room to her. I nodded to her in a curious complacency.

I watched ever so closely as she removed the covers of coffins and peered inside. "Crows. Grave robbers. Heathen barbarians." The words of so many filtered through my thoughts, and so I watched Georgetta with great interest as she examined the bones lying in their stone and wooden cradles. Each coffin lid she moved was replaced; every item and bone was carefully set back. She came at last to the hastily constructed wooden box that held the late Sevil Armre' El. Upon removal of its covering, Georgetta stood in a silent gaze at the remains. "Father Myers," she called, "I assume you've performed your church's burial rights?"

"Yes, I have performed the rights," I replied.

She bade me come over to the coffin and instructed that I stand next to it. I couldn't help it. Half a corpse stole my gaze and held on with icy fingers; the mortician had done her best. Georgetta opened a small pouch of salt, poured it onto the floor in the center of the room, and, using her finger, drew a symbol I did not recognize. As she did so, she spoke again: "You will bless the corpse again, but only at my say-so. Do you understand?"

I replied in a monotone and assuredly held my wand and water at the ready. From her belt Georgetta pulled and brandished a pendant of silver and sapphire over the mayor's body. I took in a deep breath to steady my heart. Georgetta began softly, "You whose bones from dust return to dust, I beseech grant me the wisdom your eyes now see." The pendant in her hand that had been softly swaying was now taut and motionless and put a strain in the hand of its bearer. She spoke again, softly as before, and continued. As she did, the pendant that had stopped its gentle sway to strain on her hands was now animated again, twisting and pulling in violent bursts in every direction the length of chain allowed.

I took in another deep breath and found the air stung my lungs with a harsh cold; the light of our lantern flickered and fought to stay aflame. The strangest of sounds filled my ears. A deep and distant rumbling like that of a heavy table scraping across the floor bounced and vibrated off the air, and the strangest part of it all was that it touched only the air. This sound emanating from gods knew where refused to touch the walls of our small room and lived only in the air between them. It grew in intensity at a frighteningly steady pace, morphing into what was an undeniable wailing through gritted teeth. The lantern's flame danced in and out of life, illuminating the closing walls brighter than it had any right to.

I looked to the center of the room at the salt. In the change of brilliant light and utter darkness, as the two fought for existence against each other, I saw…something. Someone. A face bodiless, gasping, gnashing, screaming! Its eyes bloodshot, never blinking, clinging to mine! Each sharp breath of cold air stung more than the last. I stood my ground, waiting and listening for Georgetta to give the command. It didn't come. Instead the air was warm again; the lantern was now shining as before with its soft, simple glow. Georgetta, breathing heavily and sweating, placed her back to a wall and slumped down onto the ground.

"As easily as one exerts themselves to push a chair, so too will any act of the Arcane exert itself onto the user. As one would use a hammer to drive a nail, so too does the human body need tools." The opening words of *Sceldaven Runes and Rituals,* volume 1, by Alejandro Du Ver'. These words became prominent in my mind as I looked upon Georgetta. I placed the lid back onto its coffin, my back to the same wall as my companion, and sat down. It was all I had to give, so I offered her the water I carried.

She eyed me a moment before taking the water and sighing. "She will not know peace until we've given her spirit justice. I would believe by killing what did this to her." She said this with the same dissatisfied expression I had seen before. Georgetta then pointed to one of the coffins. "Look at that one—tell me what you see."

I carried myself across with the lantern in hand and observed. "There are scratches on the corners," I said. "They look as though they were made from claws? Rather than the act of being placed by careless hands."

Georgetta then instructed me to open it and look inside. The bones that lay there had been mangled with various claw marks and indentions that she revealed to me as teeth marks.

"Ghouls," she said. "Ghouls are those who have tasted the flesh of the dead and fall to a never-ending hunger for it. Cursed with undeath rather than blessed, their bodies are in a constant fight with rigor mortis and so do all they can to avoid conflict. They're rarely so intelligent as to replace the coffin covers, and their skin is usually cut like butter." Georgetta rose to her feet. "The one we killed is not like any I've seen before, Father Myers. I need to examine it."

We both were standing, looking at the now-empty floor of the home, when our ears caught the sound of clamoring and yelling. We quickly made our way back to the main street and followed the rising smoke overhead. We followed the sky-rising trail to the town entry, past the wooden behemoth and steps away from the single-doored gate. The remaining denizens had dragged the ghoul out of the home and placed it upon a pyre. All people were dancing and singing and yelling; children threw stones at the corpse ablaze. We could hardly see the corpse through the drunken bodies enjoying the festivities.

Georgetta and I discussed the inevitable attack come nightfall: whether these creatures were intelligent enough to lie and wait or wrathful enough to seek revenge. In what ways might they attack again? Unable to set hand and foot on the mud of the streets, would they look for alternative means to strike? How many were they? I asked her if these creatures were typically subterranean.

"No," she replied and explained how they looked for dark places to hide but did not possess the capability of digging, as ours did. To understand these creatures, we would need another body to examine. "How do you fare with your musket?" Georgetta asked.

The fire burned for the remainder of the day. I was reminded of this each time my back hit the ground and Georgetta's voice rang, saying, "Again." In the small of the afternoon and into the diminished light, she imparted what she deemed necessary for me to learn. Grappling was particularly difficult for me to understand as each lesson was learned while the mud cushioned my fall. Falling was a skill I had not once in my time in the priesthood thought I would need or value so highly. Next was the art of fencing, practiced with two broom handles and my now-bloodied knuckles.

Perhaps it was my own temperament, the time constraint, or something else entirely that prevented these concepts from being etched into my mind. I was not defiant in my lessons; no, to the contrary, I felt an alien sensation of eagerness to learn. If these skills could help me protect the people here, then I was thankful to be learning them. Through blood and bruise and dimming light, Georgetta imparted her wisdom unto me. Even if somewhat harshly. Eventually the fire died on its own. The people returned to the haven of the hasty floors and remanned their makeshift posts.

After I had cleaned and bandaged myself, Georgetta began a new lesson. A lesson in the arcane. A lesson in magic. My books described the use of runes in detail, but my new mentor spoke of something far deeper. Of all the races in all the corners of the known world, humans had the most difficulty in the uses of magic. She spoke more softly than she had before, with a passionate, tempered respect around her words: "Magic is not a power conjured into existence at the whim of one, nor is it a vein free flowing through the world tapped into by one. It is the world. It is the very wood we now sit on and the air filling your lungs. Magic is the use of our world around us and is stagnated only by the individual's mind. You performed an impressive feat of it when you blessed the ground. It was potent and lasting."

She then reached into my bag lying beside us, spying a small shining scepter kept in a strap. She paused and glanced at me. "You are a curious one, Father Myers," she said as she then pulled the scepter from my bag. I imagined she saw the spine of my heretical choice in reading from the look in her eyes. "You chose to use thistle rather than scepter." It twisted in her hands, its copper catching flickers of lantern fire. "You have an understanding of the world so few have. I wonder what would become of you if you became a part of it." She handed my scepter back to me. The night passed slowly and silently. Fireflies flittered about the air, and the sound of crickets and frogs filled my ears for the first and only time that autumn.

I awoke staring into the deep, dark, lightless void that was the inside of my hat. The sound of coffee being poured roused my spirits and my body to an upright although stiff position. "They didn't appear last night. We will have to hunt one down," Georgetta said as she handed me a cup. She asked me what I knew of the innkeeper.

Inhaling my coffee, I told her of my interactions with the person in question. The church had paid for my room, so my interactions had been limited to her hasty exit from a conversation into her room behind the bar. For a moment we both sat in silence.

"Keep your musket with you," she said. We both stood on our questionable platform looking out over the streets at the slowly ambling people. "I want into that room. And I want to search the mayor's office," Georgetta proclaimed.

"I can lead the townspeople in prayer and blessing to give you time to search the room. I won't be able to account for any persons not interested, however. Lonut will open the office building on request," I said.

Gathering as many people as I could, we walked to the village entry, where I then stood atop the charred pyre, caving remains dusting away beneath me. People circled around me. I don't remember most of what I said except that I mentioned how brave and stouthearted the people were and that they would soon have their town reclaimed. I read passages from the book of Erëdna; all the while my attention was on the back of the crowd. At any glance behind them or an expression of lack of interest, I raised my voice. A few of the people applauded, which grew to a majority of the people, which grew to all those that had gathered. As my speech came to a natural conclusion and the others walked away, I could only hope the time I had bought was enough and that the breach of privacy was justified.

Georgetta stepped out of the inn and fished Lonut out of the crowd. Together they walked off toward the square and out of sight. After the few that had a need to be heard by me had left my ear and my path, I quickly made my way to the mayor's office. Georgetta was alone, searching the inside of the previously barred building. I went to ask what she had found, but before I could form the word "did," she interrupted: "Start searching."

"Excuse me?" I replied.

"I found what I was looking for; now I want you to find it."

I removed my musket from my shoulder and placed it near the door only to take a step forward having a blade pressed to my neck and an eyebrow raised at me. I stepped backward and slung the wood and iron across my shoulder once more. My passage across the room was now evidently open.

I rummaged through the various cabinet drawers, launching dust into the air, and found documents of the various happenings and plans of the town, many of which were dated back a decade or two and largely disagreeable to my investigation. That is, until I found a space where dust had been recently removed, more so than in other spots. Inside this drawer were parchments that hooked my eye: maps of the town layout. Leafing through the pages, I found that the town had boomed in prosperity when its mine shafts were open. There were a number of entrances, all sealed, scattered on the outskirts of the wall running for miles, according to the plans. However, one entrance was inside the town and had doubled as a bunkhouse for the miners but was later demolished to make way for an inn.

Georgetta beckoned I follow her out the door and to the inn. Eyes peered at us in astonishment as Georgetta flung open the door behind the wooden counter. There was a humble room with a bed and lectern desk and an odd amount of scratch marks on the floor near a bookcase. The innkeeper was small and frail, and as the evidence showed, had to drag the case aside, whereas Georgetta lifted one end and threw it aside with ease. Lantern light seeped out from the edges of the small old door revealed before us. Behind it was a corridor descending to the adit of the old iron mine. It was a miracle how well the bookcase trapped the smell. "We must prepare for this. Go back." I didn't hesitate; at her words, I turned and exited back through the small door.

The innkeeper stood in stunned silence and horror as we emerged. I don't know if Georgetta reacted to the woman fleeing or the woman fled in reaction to Georgetta lunging at her, but what I saw next was the body of the frail woman being snatched by the neck and lifted into the air to come plummeting down onto the bed. Georgetta drew her blade and pressed it to the neck of her captive, drawing blood.

I lashed out in anger at the sight and yelled the innkeeper's name. "Open the lectern!" Feeling a cold chill run down my spine, I dragged the bookcase back into its place and then proceeded to open the desk. In it were blank parchments, ink and pen, and three rolled letters. Each bore a blank wax seal, void of any signature.

The first letter opened with a proposition of a vague plan to reopen a mine shaft in an attempt at restoring prosperity to both the small town and the city. The writer stressed the importance of asking few questions, telling no one, and sending a reply with the same courier before he left. According to the first letter, a pouch of thirty-five copper pieces and seven silver pieces was attached, and more would come if the reply was satisfactory.

As I finished reading this letter, my dear friend the barkeep entered the room. "What the fuck are you shits doing?" he shouted.

I tried to calm him. "Please, friend, allow me to speak."

He replied by telling me to fuck myself and threw more vulgarities at me as I tried again to calm him and explain. He grabbed me by my collar. I dropped the letters from my hand and firmly planted my fist into his eye. "Shut your gods-be-damned mouth and allow me to read, you arrogant child." I think I heard Georgetta chuckle slightly then. The barkeep chose to remain silent, and in the small room he turned to find a second blade in Georgetta's hand pointed at him.

I continued with the letters. "*Your choice to aid will go greatly rewarded. However, it would be wise to continue our correspondence without the use of signatures, and if you truly have no access to a wax seal, perhaps a ribbon would better serve.*" The writer continued, explaining that the entrance under the inn must be reopened, as well as the adit to the east side. "*The tunnels will be used to transport and store the necessary materials.*" Each letter was written by a different hand. One letter bore the vaguely recognizable style and strokes of a pen and hand. In that moment I chose to ignore the evidence before my eyes. "Will she tell us anything she knows?" I asked.

Georgetta looked at the hapless woman and raised an eyebrow. The innkeeper knew little about her correspondence; she had asked no questions and had taken no action beyond instruction. She did speak of the altars, as she described them, erected in the tunnels below.

"Adalane. You're responsible for this?" The barkeep's eyes watered as he rose to his feet. He reached for the letters in my hand, and I tentatively released them, then watched as he read.

"Father Myers. We have a woman who has confessed. Her actions are the result of abominations murdering innocents. Those creatures are still roaming beneath our feet as we speak. What is your decision with her?" Georgetta, still holding the blade to the woman's skin, looked hard at us both and waited.

The barkeep, slack jawed, looked at us with a worried fever. I was thrust into a position I had no authority in. A position I believed I shouldn't have authority in. I drew a deep breath and placed my hand on his shoulder. "Go and gather the remaining officials." I turned to my companion. "It is not for us to decide what should happen."

She sheathed her sword, saying, "You can't fire the musket in the tunnels. Grab a blade and your branches."

We made haste in our preparations to venture down into abandonment. Georgetta was obviously ready at a faster pace. I had not brought nor owned a sword, and she had none suitable to spare, so through the crowd of hands pulling Adalane through the door, I grasped the shoulder of my acquaintance Lonut. I asked if there was a smith still present from whom I might procure a blade. A wave of his hand and we began walking toward his homestead. He must have seen my concerned expression as he stated with some certainty that no decision about the matter of Adalane would be finalized without him.

"What will they do?" I asked. He said he wasn't entirely sure but that again he knew no decision would be finalized without his input. He slowly pushed open the door to his home and quietly, carefully stepped on blankets laid out across the floor until he reached the mantel, where he grabbed something from up top and then made his way back to me. "It was a gift for years of service," he said. "It would serve better in your hands than it has me, collecting dust."

Lonut held out a simple cross-hilt short sword. "The leather was from a prized cow. Got old, see. The blade is sharp—'twas a hobby of mind to keep it so. Helped my mind stay like a blade itself." He chuckled to himself as he finished speaking. A bauble was tied at the end of the sheath, which he informed me was oil for the blade. He patted my shoulder and wandered off in the direction of the increasing shouting coming from the gates.

I turned on my heels to meet Georgetta back in the basement room. She had set out an assortment of items—two lanterns with oil, waterskins, dried jerky, and fruits—all of which were divided for two. Waiting for us in a corner was an onlooker from before.

Georgetta gave an expression of genuine fascination when she spied the sword in my possession. "Are you ready, Father Myers?" she asked.

"Not just yet." I knelt down on the ground, opened my bauble of oil, and from my thistle wand dripped a droplet of water into it. Carefully and sparingly I applied the oil to the blade. Gathering our things, we resigned ourselves to delve into the mine and face the horrors that plagued the very grounds. That onlooker removed the bookshelf from our path and closed it again behind us.

The rancid, putrid, vile smell made every inch forward its own test of our resolve. The light we brought was cut short by the same ghastly yellow haze, only here it was thick, like dense fog. Our steps echoed despite our careful slog down the corridors. We walked single file, Georgetta and I, across the narrow wood planks left as pathways atop the mud and jagged rock. The silence was deafening; each step was thunder, like the hammer of a god. The dripping of trickling water down the walls reverberated like a cascade of water down a mountainside. The walls, so tight, pushed the very air in on itself.

It wasn't long before our steps were elongated over half-eaten bodies left as hors d'oeuvres for the flies and cockroaches. We trod carefully, as the bodies had been dragged only feet away from or dropped directly under fresh unstable tunnels—tunnels that reached up into the foundations above. It was a miracle the town had remained aboveground rather than sinking into a horrid grave. Fractured support beams moaned and joined our prayers and blessings over the bodies we discovered. Each was given a personal prayer that came from neither tome nor scroll but from Georgetta's heart as well as mine. Given the state of their bodies and what we witnessed in the crypt, nothing else seemed fitting for these damned souls.

The mine had been abandoned and built over, as the plans to the town had revealed. What we did not understand at first was why. The answer as such made our search relatively easier: many of the lower tunnels had flooded, and as a result many more had collapsed. The ghouls' tunnels dug upward, suggesting that we would only have to travel the dry open pathways. Georgetta, ahead of me, leaned over a hole for a brief moment before continuing onward. Curiosity overtook me, and I did the same as my companion; a ladder was cresting the surprisingly clear, still water. My lantern light dancing on the walls could reveal enough of the scene below the uncertain depths. Two skeletons, one on top of the other, tools still attached to preserved clothing.

"The flooding had to have happened suddenly and quickly. One or both panicked and dragged the other down," said Georgetta. Swimming would not be a necessary skill for most inlanders.

Pushing forward, we came to a dry, steady crossroad. What had once been used as a common area for the miners to eat and drink was now being used as an altar room. Our lanterns' light flittered and danced across the walls and over the five mounds of dirt and wood circling the center of the room. We approached with caution; each step closer brought new light to our eyes. The coffins were of an unfamiliar design, adorned with carvings and writings and supported by imported stones and bedded with the mud aforementioned. Each one was empty. Five of them there were.

"These were used to create the ghouls?" I asked.

Georgetta nodded in agreement with my assessment. She grabbed a table from the ground and placed it upright. After setting her lantern down on top of it, she produced a book from her bag. It was embroidered with the image of a crow carrying parchment and had a small clasp holding the covers in place. Turning to face the surrounding tunnels, she spoke to me, saying, "Open it, please."

I was hesitant, admittedly, but I backed to the table and handled the clasp. It would not open. There was no lock to be seen, and yet no matter how I struggled to remove it, the clasp remained unmoved. Georgetta then reached back and flicked a few fingers in the air above her book, and the clasp fell open of its own accord. "You're toying with me, aren't you?" I asked. She smiled.

We would have to dismantle the altars, and she was preparing us for the task. A task I had many questions about, and she graciously provided the answers. My first query was if the destruction of the altars would stop the creatures outright. Unfortunately, the unholy mounds of decay were merely the source of their creation and did not sustain them. She then explained that we would be taking turns destroying the altars, as the acts of understanding the intent of the symbols and writing and counteracting their magics would take time and put strain on the body. I then asked if my blessing of holy water and thistle would be enough to destroy the intents of the ones who had made them. Georgetta told me that if my will was strong enough and my wand of thistle was a stout enough tool, then yes, it would work; however, the possibility of violent resistance from the altars might be enough to bring down an already crumbling mine. Neither of us was willing to take that risk.

Georgetta knelt by the first altar. Book at her side and a silver dagger in her hand, she thumbed through the pages of references, guides, and spells and slowly carved the dagger into the wood, carefully choosing a symbol here and a symbol there to deface. I paced the room, sprinkling water at the entrance and on the walls of each tunnel surrounding us in a dark risk and a circle of hopeful preservation.

As I vultured my way around the room, keeping an eye down every corridor, I became aware of a smell that persisted through the already-present foul decay. It was a chemical smell, like what I had experienced in the morgue when I first arrived and again when we examined the crypt. I didn't know it, nor was it a match to the previous odors, only reminiscent. No body emerged, no howling faces, just an odor fading away.

My mind began to wander to Georgetta's earlier teachings and the writings of Alejandro Du Ver'. "*The right tool.*" I went to a corridor and stood close to the dark blanket before me. I eyed my wand and twirled it in my palm. I wet the tip of my fingers with my blessed water, held my hand out with the same intent and want, and I flicked. The thought to do so before had never occurred to me; it was a new line of inquiry, much like the tingling sensation that ran from my fingers and shot up to my heart, wrapping itself around my beating chest and forcing the faintest involuntary gasp from my lungs. I tried again; this time, thistle in hand, I flicked water from the tips of the branch and leaves. I felt nothing. No tingle in the hands or chest, no force crushing my lungs inward. *The right tool indeed*, I thought to myself.

Georgetta had finished defacing the first altar at the time our lanterns needed new oil. The weight of the air lifted and the color retreated with each scratch of her dagger. It was now my turn. The writing on the coffins was all uniform, each symbol in the same space, the same distance from one another, every word carefully written. She gave me her dagger and her book. On a blank page she had sketched a coffin and marked the order in which she had removed the writing. She knelt down next to me and placed a hand on my shoulder. "Breathe deep and calm. Feel the ground beneath you and the air on your skin. Imagine each breath flowing from your lungs down into your legs and out into the ground like a gentle stream." She watched me deface the first few marks before standing up, wiping the sweat from her brow, and starting her patrol around the room.

It was indeed like a stream but not gentle—no, not at first. It was thrashing and bubbling as a stream does when a leaky dam is thrown across it. Patiently, little by little, carving the dagger into the wood, I released the grip that dam had between me and the outrageous box I knelt beside. The tingling that I had felt moments before was now like the sting of a wasp felt on every fiber of my body, made bearable only by the patient, cognitive breathing and its placement into the ground beneath me. I had marked out two runes and one word before the sweat began rolling down my face. This was going to take time. I was halfway through the first side when Georgetta spoke: "We have company."

The wasp sting subsided almost immediately when I stepped away to grab my weapons. I looked down the same corridor as she. There in the darkness at the edge of lantern light was a pair of glinting, coyote-like eyes peering back at us. We stood still, the three of us. The eyes glanced back and forth, first at me, then to Georgetta. "Myers, flick water at it," she said to me.

"It won't reach far enough," I replied. She insisted, and I complied. I dipped the wand in water, took a stance just in front of Georgetta, and threw the water out. At that moment Georgetta pivoted, extending her sword arm. The droplets corrected their arc downward into an arrow-like descent in speed and accuracy through the corridor! Sparks of blue flame erupted, illuminating our target, one landing in its ghastly eye. The scream that followed was shrill and piercing and echoed in such a way I would have sworn it to bring the mine down on top of us. The creature charged. As it galloped down the wooden planks, its claws flung wood chips into the air.

"On your knee!" Georgetta pushed me down and stood above me.

We both readied our blades; it leaped over the line of water, claws extended toward our flesh! Georgetta's blade struck first, digging into the chest of the beast, followed by my own sinking into its bloated stomach. Thank Erëdna I was wearing my hat. Flames crawled from the punctures, and a thick ichor dripped out, both accompanied by the fire. The shrill screams stopped. Its writhing quickly followed. The force of its lunge had pushed us both back and would likely have knocked us to the ground if not for its small size and Georgetta's strength.

I reapplied oil to my blade, knelt down, and began my work again on the altar. Georgetta ripped a few blank pages from her book and dragged the body over to the table to examine the creature and began a crude autopsy, sketching and diagramming everything she could under the light. I had to stop multiple times to catch my breath and wipe the sweat from my brow. Our rations were not enough for us to stay, and I was covered in ichor and coagulated blood. I would not be able to rest, and so I pushed through the pain. The waterskins were large; however, I lessened my takes to ensure I had more for later, seeing as we might be here for quite some time despite my efforts. Finally, I had finished my trudge around the second coffin. The haze drained of its color and intensity.

The process began again with Georgetta at a box and me patrolling the junction. On a round, I took a moment to examine the ghoul's body. Thin, leathery skin stretched over the bones so tightly the muscle and ligaments could be seen. Veins almost as prominent as roots jutted from the corpse. Its very image solicited rage and fear in me. My stomach churned; the hairs on my body refused to sit back down. This had been a person, a human being. I asked myself what could have driven these people to such depredation. Did they seek power? The favor of some demon?

"How long have you been a Crow?" I asked.

Without pause, Georgetta answered me. "Three years, and a year of training."

"Why were you sent alone?" I asked.

"The nature of our work," she replied. "Most hunters live between three to five years; the losses leave our numbers small; that first year is unforgiving."

Surely, I had thought—and I did express—that the invention of black powder weapons would perhaps prolong the life of a hunter.

Carving away at the wood, she filled the walls with her voice. In some cases, depending on the individual, these weapons had been useful, if implemented creatively enough. However, she continued, they were weighty, clumsy, and expensive, more suited to the life of a soldier. She said that for many of the terrors she had faced, by the time she was aware of its presence, it would have been too late to aim; armor and a well-trained blade had indeed served her well.

"A priest of Erëdna. Why?" she asked.

"My parents were farmers. The land was rough and poor. Too poor to raise me on. So they gave me to the church at birth. I was fortunate to visit them once as a boy before sickness took them."

Georgetta turned to me. "Fortunate."

It was my turn again. Horrid in smell as the air was, it was cold, making the feeling easier to bear. My friend refilled the lanterns, and we continued our rotations. All the while glinting eyes would appear in the tunnels, eyes without lids to close. Only the eyes were seen, the creatures dared not to step into the light. On occasion they would quickly disappear, not retreating back into the black abyss but into the ceiling. Dust would then collect on the rim of my hat, and the eyes would appear again in a tunnel behind. Low grunts and growls followed by shrilling screeches would echo between the pairs. At one point, believing it to be naught but exhaustion, I thought I heard those few grunts translate into "No…there…" I examined our dead friend for lips. Portions of the mouth had been bitten away and ripped inward, exposing rotten, jagged teeth.

Our rations had dwindled; however, our work on the altars had been completed. The air was finally clear. The moisture of the haze that clung to every surface and the very air itself had dried. That's when the coughing began. Not from myself or from Georgetta. It came from the dark. Dry wheezing jumped from glinting eyes to glinting eyes. I tried to stand, and my legs shook from the effort. With the marking defaced and the ghouls' magics deterred, we would have to either leave the mine to resupply or stay and hunt.

After a very quick and agreeable discussion, Georgetta and I decided it would defeat the purpose of our mission to return to the surface. We gathered our belongings and chose a pathway. Specifically, we chose one opposite the hollow eyes watching us and giving the appearance of descent farther into the mine. The planks moaned and creaked at each step. Georgetta was forward; I took position behind. Our advance was slow as we walked nearly back to back along a failing walkway. We passed another flooded shaft, so I took a moment to refill the bauble with water to bless. I had closed the cap and lifted my head to bring my legs to follow when the light from my belt shone back at me mere feet away in two deformed orbs. "Georgetta," I said softly.

"I have one too," she replied. Gently the bauble touched the muddied floor and in my hand replaced the wand. I dipped it into the pool, submerging my hand.

"Breathe. Watch the hands, not the eyes," said Georgetta.

Both ghouls tore the wood away when they left the ground, one leg in front of the other. I could hear nothing through the ringing of mucus-clogged screeching. Georgetta met her assailant blade to claw! I whipped my creature back with each flick of thistle, and the walls were painted with shadow and flame azure. I twisted my wrist to allow the momentum to carry off droplets of water with each step forward and back, adjusting to the distance of the horror that was hell bent on rending my flesh from my bones!

Georgetta, short sword and dagger in hand, moved as a master artist with a brush. Each lunge of the creature was met with a quick parry that sent it off balance and into the walls surrounding, followed by slashes to the neck, shoulders, and elbows! Our dance was a dire one as each advance from a creature was answered by an adjustment limited to the space left between us all. That space quickly shrank as the thistle ran dry. The distance I had managed to force between me and the corpse had become the length of my blade. I was far less adept at this than my friend, though I did succeed in blocking a swipe here and a swipe there, causing recoil in my opponent and bringing forth the bright-blue flames. Each step, block, and thrust dried my blade.

Our steps had carried us out of reach of the pool. I called out to Georgetta to make clear that we needed it, and as I did so, she took a glance over her shoulder to recapture her surroundings. At that moment, the ghoul found an opening. It stretched forward, reaching out a scarred, charred claw and dragged its hand across her torso, gashing into her armor and leaving its neck exposed. Georgetta plunged her dagger into the base of its skull, and, using all her might, flung the body back first into the wall! She followed up with a pierce of her sword to the heart and many swift strikes from her knee into its jaw, shoving the dagger farther into the damned. The brightest of blue light crackled over the body until the flames diminished. Poised behind me she stood, in front a now more agitated aggressor, the pool between my friend and me once more.

There was no time to grab the oil. The ghoul jumped forward, grasping my blade in one hand and digging the other into my shoulder. Screaming at the pain, I pushed harder than my body had any right to! Its head bent down to mine, jaws agape and salivating before its back was met with silver. Georgetta pulled, and I kicked the beast off! It fell between us, squirming and writhing. It grabbed and ripped the plank between it and the ground before it began to dig with such force and speed. It made it halfway in before I scrambled to my feet and grasped one side of its body and Georgetta the other. We lifted, pulled, and threw the screamer into the flooded shaft. I could barely see through the tears in my eyes, but the water reflected the brightest and longest flame I had yet seen. The flame sank with the body down into the clear depth.

I slumped against the wall within reach of the pool, shoulder clasped in my hand. Georgetta rushed over to me and examined my shoulder. While she looked after me, I couldn't help but try and do the same for her. She was not impressed. There was no blood coming from the slashes across her torso, large as they were. She saw the concern in my eyes and reassured me she was unharmed and that the ghoul had not gotten completely through the armor. It would, of course, need repair after such damage.

She would need to remove my coat to better see my wounds, and so, with wincing and gasps of pain, I moved away from the wall enough to remove the coat from my shoulder. The wounds were deep, and it had become difficult for me to focus. Georgetta produced a small kit of salves and bandages, but I was bleeding faster than the kit could keep up with. In a drunken manner, I pointed to that water and asked her as best as I could to pour the water over my shoulder, place my wand upon me, and utter an intent of health. I trusted that she understood far more than I about the anatomy of a shoulder in order to close the wounds properly. She did as I asked. Cool water rushed over me, and the gentle chant of her voice accompanied the placement of thistle.

I came to consciousness with the tightening of the last bandage. "There will be scarring, but you should be able to move it again soon," she said.

"Thank you," I replied.

The last of the dried fruits and meats made for a quick meal as we took stock. My bauble was shattered; the thistle had browned and wilted. Georgetta's armor was still useful, from the back at least. The lights dimmed from the exhaustion of oil; like the slow extinguishing of the lantern, we too retreated back to where we had begun. Georgetta decided I was in no condition to fight again and she would send me back up to rest. She would hunt the last all on her own, and despite my reservations, I had no doubts she would be successful.

Finally, we came to the familiar crossing, and over from our entry stood the table holding the corpse of a creature—no, two creatures, one with its eyes intently fixed on us. It crouched on all fours over the body of its like in between us and ascent to the village. It was larger than the rest, its skin yellowed enough to see even in the darkness, and amid the emaciation and mutilation protruded small spines in no natural order; instead, they existed upon its skin in patches, some of which were growing into each other.

Georgetta stood firm, weapons drawn, and placed herself between me and the creature. It crawled forward, oh so slowly and carefully reaching down to the ground. Its eyes never once moved from ours, its nails digging at the rock floor. A labored, deep breath drew into its half-moving lung, and from its jaws came *"Ww...wwhhhyyyyy?"* It didn't move. We didn't move. The air was still. From mucus-drawn breath, again the mangled horror asked us, *"Wh-whh-whh...yy?"* It turned to place a hand on the corpse's shoulder, still holding its eyes to ours.

We were all silent. Standing still, waiting for one another to move. I stepped around Georgetta and in the calmest voice I could muster asked, "Why, what?" I knew very well what it meant. I knew very well that it wanted to know why we had killed the rest of them. The look on Georgetta's face was nothing short of pure bewilderment. All I could think to do was to take advantage of a moment's peace with words.

At my question, its lungs churned in small huffs, and its body swayed as if searching for an answer. It spoke again, raspy and defiled as its voice was, and asked, *"Why...f-f-family...gone?"* Georgetta glanced at me. The creature didn't move its hand away from the other, nor did it hunch over to hide itself from strikes, but stood upright, open and vulnerable.

I answered, "Your family has killed other families, and that had to stop."

Its breath grew heavy; its deformed eyes searched the room. *"Nnooo... families...f-f-food? Tol...told...food?"*

Georgetta spoke out: "Who? Who told you they were food?"

It pointed to the altars. *"Maker..."* It turned back to the table and gently pressed its hands on the corpse, pushing as if to wake it from sleeping. With its back to us, I drew my blade and stepped forward past Georgetta, who looked me in the eye with disgust and then grabbed me and shook her head.

"It's killed almost an entire village," I said, hushed.

She raised her brow at me, moving not another muscle.

"That creature is everything my goddess stands against!"

Georgetta stood tall, looked me in the eye, and spoke: "It is no more than a lost child." The air was so cold I could feel it running down the back of my neck.

The ghoul turned to watch us. *"Where...food?"* it asked. It glanced back and forth between Georgetta and me.

She never took her eyes off mine.

"Can it eat anything besides people?" I asked.

She nodded her head once, indicating yes. I suggested the forest, west of the pass through it. Georgetta disagreed and said it was too close to the river and might be spotted by travelers and fishermen. She turned and pointed at a wall. "Dig straight for a day. There, the trees will hide you from those like us; food will be bountiful. Do not let others like us know you are there. They will not be so kind."

The ghoul looked closely at us and at the spot on the wall and back again. In the same raspy yet somehow more noticeably choked voice, it asked if its family would follow. Georgetta said it would be alone, but it would be safe. Keeping its eyes fixed upon us, it crawled over to the wall, placed its cupped claws on it, and began to dig. Rock and dirt were flung with amazing speed. We both kept our eyes on the ceiling. In moments, the tunnel was dug out of eyesight and earshot; as far as lantern light could tell, there was no deviation.

There we were, alone in a cold, dark mine. Georgetta gently bade me to follow her; so, we made our way back to the surface. It was a quiet walk. We pushed the bookcase out of our way to enter a dark room. The bedsheets were missing, and the desk had been raided of its papers. We stepped back into the lobby and were greeted with elated faces. They began cheering and chanting; some even wept tears of joy. We were rushed with hugs and kisses from all the strangers surrounding us. Some children poked at the gaps in Georgetta's armor. It was all so sudden and difficult for me to understand.

Georgetta was unfazed by the gleeful crying and admiration and instead asked to be taken to Lonut over the shouts of our audience. Some rushed out the door before us, and others followed behind. The sun was shining, bright and almost hurtful to the eyes. I looked away toward the gate; hanging by a bedspread from the inn's signage a few feet from the ground was Adalane. She swung in the gentle autumn breeze, void of any other motion. Georgetta put her hand on my shoulder. "Claws and teeth do not a monster make, but one's words and the actions that follow them."

We sat in the office building with Lonut. Coffee and bread sat untouched. Georgetta explained what had happened in the mine, describing the bodies that were there, the failing structures underneath, and the one ghoul we let go. Lonut was enthusiastic about much of the news but expressed confusion at the last part. Not hate or contempt for our actions or even for the creature itself; rather, he seemed altogether pleased that his nightmare had ended one way or another. I offered him the return of his sword; however, he insisted I keep it. With news of the mine he would try to convince the remaining people to find a new home and didn't want a reminder of his troubles. He thanked Georgetta and shook my hand and patted me on the shoulder. A stamp was placed on a parchment Georgetta produced. A form of payment or note, I gathered, but I didn't have the strength to ask. My time here had finally come to an end, and I had to return to the city.

Georgetta stood with me at the gates. "I cannot come with you to the city," she said. I nodded in reply. My words were a mess of entanglement and dared not venture from my lips. She reached into a pocket and handed me a small strip of plain blue ribbon. "Perhaps you can find who did this," she said. She had elected to stay in the village to ensure the creature would not return, to gather the tabled body for study, and to help lay to rest those that suffered still beyond our eyes.

I removed my hat and extended my arm to say my thanks to her and to say goodbye to my new friend. She grabbed my arm and pulled me in to her and embraced me in her arms. I was indeed shocked but wasted no time in embracing her as well. She told me that if in a few days I returned here and was not able to find her, I should travel east through the forest to the path's end where the fields began. From there I should go north to the first city; I would be welcomed in the Crow's lodge.

The sun had begun to set, so I gathered my things and walked. My steps were slow. The ground felt strange beneath me. The glint of flight through the canopy of trees pulled me forward through my slow slog of heavy steps. Once the village was out of sight, I again removed my hat and my belongings and tripped to the side of the path, where all at once the contents of my stomach painted the path's side. My eyes like rivers and my breath heaving, I decided to walk a few more steps, far enough away from the smell, but the shakes in my body prevented me from traveling more than a few extra feet. The fire was small; a similar-sized blanket acted as a tent. I could not sleep, no matter how tired I was. Every twitch of a twig and rustle of branches overhead sent shivers down my spine.

I put on a small pot of coffee, another gift from Lonut, and did all I could to convince my trembling body that all was over. I would go back to the city, continue as a priest, and all would be as it had been. Each thought sent shakes through my hands once more. So I sat next to my fire and blanket cover, eating a small banquet of dried fruits, impressed I could keep it down. I tried for a sip from my cup, when over the rim I saw two glinting eyes in the brush across from me. I froze in horror, looking on at the dark in wonder at what awaited me. Suddenly a rabbit jumped from the bush and paused in what must have been similar horror at the sight of me. We sat a moment in mutual terror when a twig snap behind the critter caught my attention. A coyote stood half out of the brush; the rabbit sprinted off, and the coyote followed. The eyes had gone. The calm of the wilderness returned, and the coyote and rabbit remained in my thoughts.

Shortly after sunbreak, the rain began to fall. I hid under my tent until it no longer held back the water, which was only a few minutes after the rain had begun. My hat and coat kept me relatively dry for a while as I trudged through the red mud of the pass. One hand clung to the rock wall beside me to steady my feet over the stones, roots, and puddles. The leaves above would release their pools almost as if they knew when I would be passing beneath them.

My pace, due to the weather, was incredibly slow. In many instances I had to stop entirely and take shelter beneath a rocky overhang, at which point I would fill my pot with rainwater and make more coffee. Obviously, the wood was soaked through, making it difficult to light a fire. I took the time beneath my earth-given shelter to read more from my current favorite book. My memory of Georgetta lighting a candle with nothing but her hand stuck like a thorn in me. I found a passage that mentioned the dangerous applications of even attempting the use of magic to create or manipulate fire, as fire itself is unpredictable and calls a great will to tame it. I found this to be somewhat ridiculous because if fire was so much a threat, then every hearth or lantern was an accident waiting to happen. Nevertheless, I approached my new mission with what at the time I assumed was caution and respect.

The Sceldaven, among many cultures, used runes as the book described to make their will physical and applied these to a large variety of tools and tattoos. Given the current condition of the weather, I assumed the potential rogue spark would do little harm. I found a sizable stick that fit well in the palm of my hand, and using a stone, I carved one rune into it that was supposed to represent fire—with no apparent success. I had a stick with a word I barely understood and felt much like a fool would in a court of the dead-eyed witless, waving my new wand around frantically to silence and eventually utter failure.

Reading further, I gathered that the use of runes themselves was not the key to my success, as, from my understanding, runes were largely contextual and held little power for those who did not comprehend their meanings. The Sceldaven were simply more notably successful at using writings to their advantage in such a way. I flipped through the pages for references to the ignition of a fire, and in addition to my already-carved symbol, I added words meaning *flame* and *ignite* in my Ru'vartien dialect. The volume I possessed was rather vague about whether using single words or passages would be more successful but placed a great importance on the individual and in some cases suggested that there might be no need for writings at all. I again assumed it would be safe to try to ignite a fire with writing, having a clearer written intent now.

Wand in hand, I harkened back to words of my friend Georgetta, held the wand over the pile of stones and twigs, and breathed. For the first few tries I felt nothing at all, but after changing my process of thought for a fourth time, I felt a gradual buildup of that all-too-familiar stinging sensation trickling through my body. I focused on the pile of wood and controlled my breathing, when all at once the wand burst in my hand, sending splinters through the air at incredible speeds! Many of those splinters lodged in my hand, and a few left blood dripping down my cheek, and my breath was now involuntarily heavy.

I decided to try again. I removed the splinters from my hand, wiped the blood from my cheek, and this time, rummaging around the forest floor, I found a stick almost as large as I. The rain had not let up. Using my blade as carefully as I could, which was not an easy task, I carved the same writings into the staff and positioned myself over the twigs. Again, a few tries in, and no success; however, then the sting returned to me, this time moving in slow, almost gentle waves through me until I felt them retreat into my staff. I watched as it began to dry, the water escaping at the seams and bubbling out. The pile in the stones began the same process, expelling the water within and becoming dry as a desert day. The twigs in my pile burst violently into flame with force enough to move many of the twigs out of place a foot; my staff followed their lead. The spot in my hand crumbled as the ends of the staff were consumed in fire. The bottom fell into the pile—just as well; I would use that one to heat my coffee—but the top came crashing down onto me! The sleeve of my jacket dried almost instantly. I would have been set ablaze had it not rolled off as I moved away in fear. The fiery branch rolled just out into the rain and for a time stayed alight, the ground around it steaming as it dried and became wet at the same time before eventually fizzling out.

I repeated this process as I could throughout the day, stopping at any suitable shelter, as few as they were. With each attempt I grew physically and mentally exhausted and was only made more so by the continuing rain. I had to stop entirely, as a portion of the path in front of me was under rushing water. Rather than climb around it, I resigned myself to practicing my building of a camp. Despite my exhaustion, the shakes in my hands and trembles in my mind kept me from closing my eyes, so I read more and practiced more when I had the energy. I drank all the coffee I had been given, which in itself was not a large accomplishment; I had been given only enough to last a day at the most, and I found its bitter strength an odd and effective comfort. With the rain and my continued stops, the sun had begun to set where the storm clouds met the bases of the trees.

My fire was again small, producing enough heat to cure the last of my coffee and enough light for me to strain my eyes at the book's pages. I lay on my patch of ground, blanket cover set angled above me, willing myself to close my eyes and sleep. Alas, each moment of darkness behind my eyes only sent tremors down my spine and flashes of eyes through my thoughts. The eyes hid behind the pews of Cathedral Gregori. In the high windowed walls of the abbey, a howling face hid in the cracks and crevices. Both of my assailants followed me down the corridors, jumping from shadow to shadow. As I would turn one way, I would be met with one of the creatures and turn to run another way. Each time I closed my eyes, I would find solace and safety behind one of two doors until I would wake drenched in sweat.

I slept just long enough for the fire to continue burning as if it had been lit minutes before. I decided then would be a good time to practice more, but I did not want to venture into the dark rain seeking a large enough branch for fear of meeting a sudden drop, common for these parts.

Instead, I held my hands over the small flames. I watched the light flicker about, casting shadows against the palms of my hands. I watched intently. If what it took to manipulate the world was an understanding of it, then would the possibilities not be limited to my imagination?

I recalled how in one excursion to the forbidden section of the library, which I was removed from so often, I had read a passage from a text by a dwarven scholar. It suggested that light, all light, was physical, and darkness was the absence thereof. If the shadow of my hands above was me, obscuring the flow of light in the way a damn blocks a river, could I not hold the light? I held my hands close to the flames without burning, and I focused on the light lapping around the edges. I steadied my breathing, slowed my thoughts as best I could. Slowly, ever so slowly, a stinging sensation began to fill my fingers, trickling down into my wrists.

As I had steadied myself in the pain of the altars, I steadied myself here, allowing the feeling to rush over me, embracing it to see the light under my hands grow brighter and brighter and brighter still. I found myself flushed with light disproportionate to the fire emitting it. Slowly I removed one hand—no change—and the other hand I turned over to face upward. Sitting in my hand, without weight or texture, was a shimmering ball of orange-and-white light. I could almost feel warmth spreading through me as a smile volunteered to escape. I waved my free hand through the ball, passing it back and forth, shooting shadows of peculiar shape into the walls and branches around me. I changed the position of my hand around the ball to see if it would fall to the ground, and to my surprise it fell a few inches until I jumped in fear at losing my accomplishment; I willed its rise back to my hand. At this astonishing self-discovery, I removed my hands from the light entirely and kept the sphere afloat by thought alone.

My lungs contracted, my face twinged, and a feeling I never thought to experience myself reared its head. A wheezing, violent cough forced its way through my throat. The ball exploded in the most gentle of ways, and the light disappeared. I covered my mouth until I was done being betrayed by my own body, then removed my hand and saw a few drops of blood. *Ironic*, I thought to myself.

The morning came accompanied by lighter rain. The walk would have been swifter if not for the pain in my chest that gratefully loosened its grip as the morning grew older. It was not long before the walls came into view through the mist, rising high into the air. I stopped for some time. Normally the walls of Târgaiova would inspire me with feelings of awe. All I felt was a chill running down my neck. I was tired, and the rain must have slipped down my jacket. The light of the lone gate watchman shone through a small, stark porthole. I beat my hand against the gate door and called out.

"Eh? Who goes there!" came an old tired voice. A pair of eyes peered out the window. The top half of the watchman's door slowed its way outward; a hand and lantern led a sneer out the half-open door. "Who is it that come asking?" said the man.

"Sutlor, is that you?" I asked. I was taken aback by his unusual demeanor toward me. "It's Father Myers," I exclaimed.

He leaned back and held the lantern higher. "Jaccob, be that you? Erëdna bless my eyes, I hadn't recognized you. You needn't bother bringing the soup no more. One of the sisters took it up in your absence." The hatch closed before I could utter another word. The wall did nothing to block the rain, so I stood outside waiting for my old friend to open the door. It took so long that I began to think he had forgotten we spoke. The gate door then swung open, and instead of being greeted by my friend, I was rushed in by a guardsman, who closed the gate behind me.

The streets smelled the way I liked: the scent after sunbaked brick met water. The bells chiming at the shipyard carried through the narrows between the pressed, tall buildings. I followed the well-trodden paths back to the one building that towered over the rest, higher even than the walls. Cathedral Gregori. The square in front of its large, looming doors was empty; aside from the sound of water streaming down to the sewers and the pitter of droplets on brick, it was dead quiet. So quiet my ears would not stop ringing. The shakes in my hands came in almost violent waves. Trying to steady myself, I spied a drain bubbling water out of it and something else. A faint yellow haze mixed with the water. I tore my eyes away and shut them and clasped my hands in one another. Once I had steadied, I looked back at the drain. No haze. No yellow.

I had always liked the rain. It made the city quiet. Not quiet like the hushed halls of the abbey but quiet in a peaceful, calm sense. I don't know how long I stood in the square looking up at the doors with that chill running down my spine. I'd catch ill should I stand outside any longer, so I ventured up the steps to the doors and reached out. Never had I hesitated at them. No matter the time of day or who was performing a sermon inside, I would walk into the entry as anyone would entering their home. I had never looked at the doors before, never noticed the cracks and chipping in the work. It was strange, seeing the image of Goddess Erëdna, arms outstretched, light from fingertip to fingertip beaming outward and cracked. How long had it been since the doors were cared for?

The noise of another person leaving the safety of their home behind me startled me enough to whip around and grasp the hilt at my side. I watched as they hurried out of sight on some unknown mission. I decided to enter the abbey through one of the sides. My footfalls bounced and carried through the brick. A small array of monks and sisters hastily walked by, some of them clutching texts, others prayer beads; some simply did not make eye contact. Everyone here had somewhere to be, and it was always the same place.

Finally I reached the door to my domicile. A single room with a bed, desk, trunk, and small washbasin; the coatrack had been removed. I sat on the edge of my bed. There was no window, only four walls packed together and a framed depiction of my goddess, Erëdna. I looked at nothing but my hands as they shook uncontrollably; my breath followed shortly and quickly. I had filled the basin and was slowly washing the water over my face when from behind me a voice boomed across the walls, "Jaccob, my boy."

Bishop Gregory stood in the doorway, filling the space almost entirely. I hadn't heard the door open. The light of the high hall window shone down to silhouette his shoulders as the candlelight reflected off the gold-trimmed robes in which he was adorned. "Sister Mihaela had whispered to me of your arrival from—" He ducked his head to enter the room and looked me over with a strong expression. "Perhaps they should rename it Mudtown," he said with a low disdain. He placed his candle on the desk and turned to exit the room. "I will be with the duke. We have a meeting. Clean yourself and see Sister Mihaela. I look forward to speaking with you on my return. Your coatrack will be returned to you as well."

I never before realized how much light came from the outside window as when Bishop Gregory stepped from view. I listened for each careful step he took, so close to the doors with so much weight in them, until their thunder faded into the distance.

There was an extra set of garments in the trunk. I didn't know who they belonged to. My hat was not allowed within the halls, and so it joined my bag and blade and musket beneath my bed. I pulled my hair back, tied it, and brushed my beard by the basin; one had to be presentable to speak to the sisters.

The walk to the opposite side of the abbey was long and gave me plenty of time to ponder the blue ribbon in my hand. In all my time sneaking into the forbidden section of the library, I had not read or seen anything that matched the symbols of the altars in the mine. Then again, I hardly strayed too far into the shelves for fear of being caught.

My thoughts then strayed to Mara; I supposed she had never found the courier, or I would have received word. Perhaps I would have been able to find the mine entrance used to smuggle the creatures? No, the rain had slowed me on a path already washed away; I would have gotten lost or swept under. Perhaps the courier was alive and well within the city walls? Mara wouldn't have found a trace of him on the path had he been fine, especially with so many to look after. Were they still here in the city?

Suddenly the smell of chemicals broke me from my thoughts, smells so similar to those of the village morgue but mixed and smothered by the waft of incense. I opened a door to find sisters tending to the ill and wounded. The smell overwhelmed me, and that cough I had experienced on the path leaped its way through my lungs once more, violently projecting blood into my hand. I quickly hid and wiped the blood on the backside of my robe. Many of the sisters glared at me, stopping entirely what they had been occupied with. Backs straight, not a word spoken, with the cold piercing eyes of quick judgment.

A voice called out through the barricade of people from the far inside wall. Sister Mihaela stood in a doorway, beckoning me through it. The way through the sick and those tending them felt like a long voyage across the leviathan sea. The heads of the aforementioned turned with each step I took in order to keep their eyes upon me, looking for a weakness. Sister Mihaela stepped aside to let me through and closed the door behind us. The room was sparsely furnished save for an organized desk, a chair, and a statue bearing the visage of Erëdna.

"Strip," she said impatiently. And so I did; I removed all articles of clothing and stood in the center of the room. Her eyes and hands went directly to my shoulder, the touch of which sent pain through me. Her eyes were more active than those in the hall outside but had a more distinct harshness to them. "And who did this?" she queried, still prodding my shoulder.

I calmly explained that a healer had done the work, and before I could finish the sentence, the back of her hand met my cheek. "A Crow healer," I corrected. She huffed excitedly, produced a scepter, and began raining me with water. It was cold; I did my best not to react to it but couldn't help shivering. She began to look me over once more and stopped in silence upon seeing the palms of my hands.

For a brief moment I dared not look her in the eye. She was calm and gentle. "Tried to tend your shoulder yourself, did you?" she asked. "Before that Crow could lay its hands on you."

"Yes," I replied, choking back the events of reality. It was a far better explanation.

"Tell me everything. The motives of the rat may become clear, and we will understand why it thought it might take a devout of Erëdna."

Steadying my breath as best I could, I told of my days at the village, the attacks, the people, and the events in the mine. I gave forth my explanation of blessing the grounds and how effective it was: "One of the creatures had leaped at me from a home, digging its claws into my shoulder, but died shortly after touching the ground and was burned."

Sister Mihaela was unmoved. She sat at the far wall and listened as I explained in my sundered state that help had been necessary and time had been of the essence; therefore I had not been able to send for the church. "Odd there were no messengers in the village," she said with a perplexed look upon her face. "They left with the group that came here?" she asked.

"As far as I am aware, yes, Sister," I replied. She bade me continue. I spoke of how Georgetta and I had worked together in the mine.

Mihaela sat looking at me intently and silently; the candlelight flickered in a reflection in her iris. She spoke: "You lost your scepter in the attack and tried to heal yourself without? I didn't realize you have been studying anatomy. None of my books are listed under your name or have gone missing."

My throat caught at her words. "It was a leap of faith, Sister Mihaela. I was losing too much blood," I replied.

"This would explain the witch's cough, then?" she asked.

I nodded and gave the customary answer. "Yes, Sister Mihaela."

She was silent once more and for a long while. She then extended her foot. "Kiss," she commanded. I knelt to one knee, took her foot in my hand, and kissed it.

"You may dress," she said and watched ever more intently as I replaced my robes over myself. I then went to the statue of Erëdna and kissed its feet.

The sisters continued their examinations of those in beds. "Still the favorite, I see," one said without directly addressing me.

I hurried out to a small courtyard filled with crape myrtle trees surrounding an effigy of Erëdna. I sat on a bench and held the ribbon in my hand. I couldn't breathe, and I began to sweat as I stared into the lifeless eyes of the cold stone face looming far above me. I heard nothing but the chatter of passersby in the far distance and the shuffling of sisters and monks, all stopping at the foot of the statue to pay their respects before carrying on. I watched each person bow or kneel and crane their neck forward, all fondling sets of beads adorning their shoulders. I looked up once more. The eyes that had been so hollow before seemed now to have sunken farther inward, and they had turned down to meet mine. I felt a warm burning sensation that rose from the ground up around me like a wave crashing through to pull me into a boiling sea.

I ran out of the courtyard and stopped in an alcove where I thought no one could see me catching my breath. I pocketed the ribbon, went to retrieve my hat, and exited the abbey. I wore a visage of simple meandering as best I could and made my way to the gate I had entered the city from, clutching my own set of beads and mumbling to myself while looking down every alley and through every window I passed until I eventually reached the night-shrouded gate.

There was a different watchman inside. Despite the change in face, I asked if they had been on duty and seen any travelers from the town beyond the gate. Refugees, I described them as, hoping to spark a distinction in memory. Alas. the one watching had not seen anyone pass through. I then asked when the one previously on duty would be back again, and the watchman responded with a brisk answer of uncertainty. He didn't know, so I asked who would. He would not answer for some reason, which was strange, given that they had no working schedule and delegated the duties among themselves. "Might I ask when Sutlor will be returning, then? I'd like to know when I can bring him his daily soups he was so fond of," I said.

I was met with the closing and latching of the door. A new wave washed over me, carrying the scent of decay and making my blood boil. I managed to calm myself, though the shakes didn't quite stop. Perhaps I would try an inn or a tavern this time. There were two inns that came to mind, one only up the street from where I was and one at the river docks. I doubted Mara would have wanted to stay in Târgaiova for long and might have sought to find passage on a ship. I would not be able to gather information on the messenger if they had all already left, but I would at least have some small peace of mind.

I entered Saint Aroura's Inn. Sparse of decoration and lighting, the inn had clearly not used its profits for anything other than general upkeep despite its clear traffic. All those enjoying a corner fire and more loitering in an empty lounge rushed to pay their respects to the priest who graced their door. This was after their faces turned from sour to reverent at realizing my affiliations. The innkeeper answered my questions happily, ending or beginning each sentence with "Yes, Father" or "No, Father." Unfortunately she had not seen any sign of the caravan either.

Before turning to leave, I led with another query she was all too happy to answer. "A large, rounded man with stubble." I repeated the description of a horseman to myself while wandering down to the docks.

He had often turned this way; the innkeeper informed me after returning through the gates. A few passing and pious passersby were all happy, as well, to answer my questions regarding their sightings of the man. All who recognized the description had pointed to the docks, and a few specifically pointed me to the Keelhauled, so I made my way down to that rustic inn/pub. Its walls were lined with the trophies and wonders from many a voyage out to river and sea. Jawbones and skeletal forms from creatures I'd never have imagined nor read about, mementos from lost local sailors, and stains I'd rather not take time to ponder. The chairs were filled with the weathered and weary eyed, most of whom decided to pay me little mind, as they were all engrossed in their drinks and conversation and seemed to care little about who walked through the door. Lucky for me, one man was enjoying his drinks quite loudly. At the end of the bar, a large, rounded man with bad stubble bellowed out nonsense to the bartender.

I sat down next to the odorous man, thinking of how to approach the subject of my missing persons. Had he known about the letters he carried? Was he complicit in their delivery? Had he seen my friend? A thick, heavy hand slapped me on the back, followed by a deafening juvenile laugh. "Eh, boys! They're coming for our drinks now, too, ain't they? What's its pleasure?" the man bellowed out.

Every head swiveled our way. Taking a moment, I glanced out at the now-silent crowd of sailors and warehouse backbreakers.

I turned to the tapster. "Might you have a coffee? And anything my new friend would like as well." The man's eyes widened with delight; the tapster chuckled, then asked if I wanted any spices with that. Not completely understanding him, I nodded a fain confident yes. The tapster placed a hot, steaming coffee in front of me, reached under the bar, uncorked a bottle, and then poured it in. I sat hoping it wouldn't ruin the flavor of my new favorite drink. It didn't. The intent crowd seemed pleased with my delight at the warmth of the contents of my mug and went back to their solemn conversations or lack thereof. The courier nodded for another flagon of what he had already had too much of.

Our conversation began rather abruptly, calm and without slurring of words, when I asked about the missing travelers. His eyes shifted about the room, and he leaned in to lower his voice, only for a moment, to tell me that no, he had not seen them. It was at this that he held my eyes in his, unblinking. "Eighteen beers in one night don't come with a courier's salary, Father." He went back to his laughter and smiles, to ignore my prying query.

Keeping my hand close under the bar, I removed the ribbon from my pocket. He grew silent once more. "Now, that's one question too many," he growled. I pocketed the ribbon and thanked the man for his time. I cupped his free hand in mine as I did. It was rough, calloused. I've come to understand that I know little of the world around me; however, I found this atypical of what his hands should be like. The reins of a bridle should not leave cuts and calluses like those he had. As if he had been spending his days in a warehouse, neglecting the use of gloves. I took notice of his smell once more before leaving—a terrible smell, to be sure, but one consistent with alcohol and the dust of the road rather than the sweat and brine of the docks.

I placed some copper coin in the tapster's hand and went out to the street. I still knew so little and had now grown weary. I had to convince myself it was right to allow myself rest. Perhaps after sleep I would see another route to take. Eighteen beers. The man must have had the constitution of a whale.

I walked the halls of the abbey. It was dark and lit only by the occasional candle and the light shining down from windows too high to see out of. The sound of my footsteps beat against my ears, drowning out my attempts at thought. I was tired, my body replaced with a log made of aches and sores. Finally I opened the door to my room. On my bed, laid out carefully, was a large red coat adorned with a shoulder cape fastened together with shining silver buttons. Seated in my chair, smiling against the singular candlelight, was Bishop Gregory.

"My boy, welcome back. Have a good time at the docks, did you? Seeking to bring to the light a pagan woman and her followers even when they cannot be found. Most pious indeed, Jaccob. Sister Mihaela told me everything—how you helped not one but two blasphemers see the light of Erëdna, one of those women being a flea-ridden Crow. That is most impressive for such a young father. Many in your position would beg for the chance to lead a village parish, yet you've delivered an entire people the word of the church, saving them from the consequences of their actions and being devoured by their decisions."

The bishop reached to his side and pulled forward the blade gifted to me by Lonut. "Like the crusaders of days past that fought back the night hordes, securing the human race a place on this earth. Did you know that in some places of the continent there are those that still have to fight and cower behind high walls from the shadows that seek the flesh of man? Of course you do—you've taken so many of my…research materials…I would imagine you understand how important our work is. You've seen it firsthand, no less."

He placed the blade on the bed next to the coat. "As for your actions, starting tonight you are no longer a priest. You, Jaccob Myers, are a cardinal and will be the instrument of salvation across these lands. You are to travel the world and spread our message. I have never been more proud of you, my boy. Many have already begun talking about the construction of a church in that muddied hole. Well done." He stood to walk past me, placing a hand upon my cheek. "This, of course, will always be your home." He gave my cheek a small pat and walked out.

Odd was his scent as he moved—familiar, strikingly chemical, and masked by incense. I sat in silent awe at the coat in front of me. My lungs fought against me, my hands betrayed me, and seeing the sword that lay next to the coat, I decided to look under my bed. The musket was gone. From my bag, my book had been removed as well.

I had memories of incense upon incense used here from as long ago as my boyhood. Never had I, or as far as I knew, been to the mortuary. The smell I had first been introduced to in the village, then again with each ghoul we faced. Now, it followed the man who had raised me, who had built me to be who I was. Why did it follow him? There was no reason to torture people so. I sat in silence. I couldn't accuse the man. Even under private circumstances, I had not the right to ask him. He would certainly be in his chambers the latter part of the night. If I was seen walking the halls so late, I would be questioned. "Been taken by the shadows, have you?" they would say. It had happened to so many.

But I had a new coat. A cardinal's coat. No one would question me—a cardinal, the crusader of Târgaiova—especially at these hours. The shadows of the open night were treacherous even to the pious worshipper, after all. No one would dare test their faith against the church. Most would bow their heads to me and kiss my hand. I needed only to avoid those such as Sister Mihaela and the bishop himself, those of higher stature. Those free to roam. The coat was large, heavy, but fit well. My hair flowed over the tall collar; the silver buttons gleamed in the candlelight. I placed my hat upon my head and strapped my blade to my side.

My first visit was to Târgaiova mortuary. A cold, damp, dark precipice of a building on the far edge of an expansive cemetery. My lantern cast shadows away from the family sigils and names of long-dead knights, nobles, and farmers alike. The details of inscription and quality of stone varied drastically, though despite one being a farmer or a bishop, each headstone was placed within inches of the other. The only exceptions were the multitude of mausoleums holding the far nobler and far richer names. Even these dared not climb higher than the feet of Erëdna as her stone visage towered over the center of it all, facing outward to the city.

I'll admit my imagination wandered with me each step at the poor souls mere feet beneath my own. Had they been accepted into the grace and light of the cold stone guardian watching over their rest? Had they been cast away by her into the depths of a lightless burning? The thought of either outcome brought no comfort to me.

Ahead by an arm's length now was the mortuary door. Locked. I examined the barrier closely and found no hole where a key would be inserted.

Perhaps a pull bar on the other side kept the door closed; someone, then, would be inside. I first knocked on the door to find no change in its position. And again, twice more, I knocked to find that the door remained unmoved. *A pull bar*, I repeated to myself. That should prove easy enough. I strapped my lantern to my belt and placed my palms firmly against the door. My breath drew deep as I closed my eyes. In and out the air went until all the sound of wind passing and the cry of cicadas had ceased in my ears. My hands burned with the sting, and my chest followed. The door grew in my hands. I felt each grain of wood, every chip and splinter lost to time, until I could touch the cold rust of the iron rests holding an equally old, splintered bar. One last inhale. The bar split in two as the door swung so violently it returned to me after hitting the inside wall.

A pitiful yelp came from the darkness beyond. I pushed the door aside and stepped in. A hunched, frail man with a sunken face stood in the center of the room clutching a set of prayer beads wrapped around a lighted candelabra. He stood barefoot in a nightgown. "Ease, my friend." I raised my lantern. The man's quivering changed in forms of fear as he dropped to his knees in front of me, grasping my hand. He begged for my forgiveness in small snivels, exclaiming he believed the dark had come to claim him. My mind flashed with the image of Sister Mihaela as the man knelt before me. "Stand." My voice shook as I bent down to help the man to his feet. His fear then turned to amazement. I asked his name.

"Joshua, Your Grace."

I apologized to him for the scare he had endured and explained I had come looking for answers to an important question. He was all too happy to oblige and offered to put on a pot of tea. "No, Your Grace. I ain't seen a ribbon of that sort. Don't get any letters nohow. Only messages come from the sisters or the guard. Only ever about a new body to be buried."

We stood in the supply closet as he spoke more. That smell. That chemical smell filled the air. "Do you receive any visitors?" I asked.

"Oh, almost never, Your Grace. Expect the odd guard or sister lately. The oddest thing, a guard captain—one of the duke's personal, it seemed—wasn't keen on giving his name, had been down once or twice to ask about my embalming process, much as you are, as well as a sister from the church. Tireen, I think she was. Has everyone come to run me out of my living?"

They didn't take the chemicals Joshua had on hand. Further questions led to the understanding that both visitors had asked only about the embalming and hypotheticals of different mixtures. He didn't remember what they had asked to mix them with, just that the mixtures had the potential to be volatile if done incorrectly. One last detail he gave before my departure was that of the two, the sister had watched Joshua conduct his work and took notes.

There I stood in the cemetery once more, illuminated by no more than the lantern in my hand. The rays cascading off the moon did incredibly little to help my eyes navigate the waves of stone and memories. They did, however, draw my attention up the statue. Our eyes met, and I felt cold. Alone. I walked past headstones and mausoleums once more to reach the edge of the small brick wall meant to keep the dead separated from those living in what, I saw now, were slightly larger boxes. At the realization, a brief moment of intrusive thought forced my head to turn back. The statue's eyes met mine once more. They were sunken, hollow, and contradictorily full of life. They shone brightly with a light that cascaded over the sea between us. "Stop me, then." The words surprised me as they left my lips. One blink, and the head had, without notion of movement, swiveled back cityward.

Meeting a captain of the guard would undoubtedly raise suspicion. A meeting as such was often overseen by officials. I would first have to be introduced before demanding answers. To Sister Tireen it was, then. The only ones allowed to be awake at this hour were the monks tasked with transcribing text. Those few wandering the halls to fetch water or wine rather than hunching over a desk bowed their heads to me and placed themselves against the wall until my passing.

My hands trembled. My breath shook. Before me was the door to the sisters' dormitory. Before my hand made contact, the door opened. Standing on the other side was Sister Mihaela. She looked me up and down for a brief moment before she stiffened and then bowed to kiss my hand. It took every fiber in my being to keep my hands from trembling and recoiling. "I wish to speak with Sister Tireen," I said.

"This is irregular. Even for her visits. May I inquire as to what this is about?" She stood tall.

"No. You may not," I replied.

She did not move; neither did I. We stood, testing the other's resolve. "She is sleeping," said Sister Mihaela.

"Wake her," said I.

She bowed her head again, pivoted, and turned into the dark. Moments later, she reappeared with a young sister. I instructed her to walk with me, sending a glare to Sister Mihaela as she attempted to follow behind us. We walked in silence until we were out of earshot and eyesight; then I began to question her. I began with a cough. The same guttural, blood-filled cough that had accompanied me on the road. This was far less violent, however—more an inconvenience with coloring from my lungs. "The mortuary. Tell me why you have been visiting and asking questions," I demanded.

The girl confidently contemplated my demand. "No," she replied. "The duke and the bishop would be very interested to hear about your witch's cough; that is, unless you beg me for forgiveness of your blasphemy in the name of Erëdna and pledge yourself to me." She extended a foot out. I silently refused. With a smile she turned and began walking away.

The right tool. A steady, strong instrument to place my intents through and out of. My hands stung as I grasped the hilt of my blade. The energy wrecking its way through my system traveled out of my fingertips and vibrated from the pommel to the tip of the blade. It felt uneven, but stronger than the branches from the road, aimed more like an amateur archer. Sister Tireen lifted off her feet and flew back with such force that I felt the rushing air as she flailed passed me. She was trying to scream. The impact forced out the air when she landed. Her eyes were bloodshot, her face was bruised, and the sound that simply could not escape her was nothing short of terror. The light began to leave her eyes. I had almost killed her in trying to make a point. She now lay on the floor, bloodied and bruised, and I had not even placed a hand on her. She began to weep.

I sheathed my sword and knelt down to her. "Speak, and I will call for aid," I said.

A voice called from behind me, "Aid has come." Sister Mihaela had followed. She was stern and calm and knelt down to the girl as well. With her prayer beads in hand, she touched the girl's face and wiped the blood away. Her pain eased, and the bruises slowly began to fade. "Is this what you want to be? Like them?" she asked.

My heart grew heavy as I looked upon the girl. I didn't know what to think or what to say. "What do you know?" I asked Mihaela. We were both quiet. My hands trembled so hard I felt the shocks in my chest.

"It was the guard captain that approached her. I assumed it was a simple infatuation that she had for him, but I kept an eye on her all the same. She seemed to lose interest in him, but their visits soon became more frequent. She would meet with him after returning from the mortuary to speak. She often handed him parchment and scribbles each time. I once confronted her about it, and she refused to acknowledge my position. She presumed to replace to me after a year of being in service to the church. That same night I was visited by guards in my chamber instructing me to leave the girl alone. I went to the bishop, and he assured me I would not be harmed so long as I didn't interfere."

Sister Mihaela looked over at me. "The bishop had been having dreams. Claimed the goddess spoke to him in the night. That's when he began visiting the duke. That's when the guards visited my girls."

I interjected, "The city guard had begun joining sermons and brandishing the visage of Erëdna on their armor. Was this the same time?"

She nodded her head yes.

"Have you seen any of those parchments tied with a blue ribbon?" I asked.

"Yes," she replied, "the captain would meet with a large man, a courier, after returning from the village and hand off a blue-ribbon-tied letter."

"I need to know what those letters say."

She shook her head. "There was a time where even the bishop of a church understood their place with a sister. So much has changed. He will undoubtedly have protection." She placed her hand on my shoulder. "You were always such a good boy, Jaccob. Make things right again by our Goddess Erëdna."

I was struck by several conflicting emotions, emotions I had no control over. Emotions I could not name. I stood. "Erëdna has failed us. I will do what I can by my own will."

A light flickered from underneath the lip of the double doors, battling against the light from my own lantern to claim the space shadow owned. Was the bishop gone? Was he inside? What would I say? My palms hardly understood the texture of the door as it pushed inward, revealing a lavish, large room. I'd been here before, of course, as a boy under Gregory's tutelage, though I probably could have counted on a hand the amount of times I'd seen the inside. The doors squealed on their hinges both inward and again as they swung closed behind me with an echoing bang.

It wasn't long ago I had looked in to see a large, expansive yet near empty room. The walls that now divided the space were decorated with tapestries and trinkets that would have spent a farmer's living at the dock markets and were a jarring surprise. On a small end table before me flickered the candle, illuminating the paths on either side. Seeing the beckoning of another candle's light dancing across the walls and floor, I followed it into a study. Shelves of books and scrolls lined the walls encompassing a table with another candle in the center of the room. Drawers skirted the ends of the table, similar in design to the doors guarding the entrance and similar locks to an untrained eye as mine.

The bishop is right handed; this came to my mind as I stood over the drawers. So I reached out and pulled the first one on the top right. It came loose and out easily. Sitting in the bottom, filing upward, was a stack of papers topped with a few strands of simple blue ribbon. I sat down and began to read the horribly familiar handwriting. Correspondence had been exchanged before that in my hands, which had led to the correlations to the innkeeper. Copies of the letters had been kept. Detailed copies, with notes, dates, times, and personal thoughts as to the trustworthy nature of the recipients. The notes were written by two sets of hands and suggested an exchange of the copies. The trusting, gullible nature of the village recipient was remarked upon many times with a suggestion of an increase in payment for their silence. A flaunting increase in pay with the intention of recovering the money after they passed away in the events or fled here for safety. The writings then went on to discuss the potential and viability of transformation of the individual on arrival. The five coffins had been made specifically for the process, and a stress on asking few questions was given after. With a newly reopened and resealed entrance, the mine was used to cart the coffins in, but no mention was made as to where they had originated, only where to take them. The letters stated that verbal instructions from the courier would be given after the delivery.

I was sitting uneasily, with my head in my hands, when the sound of boots shattered the silence around me. In the doorway stood a well-dressed, armored man pointing a musket at my head. "You're quite the busy man, it would seem," he said.

"Couldn't sleep. Nightmares take me," I responded. "I've not seen you hold a musket before, Captain. I took it you preferred the blade."

He looked me over and smiled at the present irony. It was a soft, respectful irony. "Consider this your official invitation," he said.

I shook my head in denial and replied, "Powder. Patch. Ball. Primer." I rose to my feet and breathed deeply.

His eyes flickered. "A pleasure then, Cardinal Myers." His hands squeezed the trigger. Nothing. He squeezed again.

"Where is the bishop?" I asked. He squeezed once more. "Is the duke involved? Where do they go?"

He did not answer. Instead, while examining the musket, he elected to say the words "peasants' craftsmanship." Calmly he placed the musket on the shelves to his side and drew his sword. On his first step forward, I coughed. Blood filled my hand until I had regained control of my breathing once more. The captain's eyes widened, and he froze.

"Where is he?" I asked once more.

The captain leaped forward to thrust his blade across the table into my chest! The blade slipped from his hand before his step made contact with the ground, and he screamed as the force of the sword's fall cracked a bone. It fell so hard that it neglected to bounce once hitting the ground.

"Where?" I growled.

He turned to run, but unfortunately for him, the weight of an already-heavy object proved to be easily manipulated. Blood spilled from his face as his chest plate rammed him down to the ground, whipping his head into it. He was still conscious as he flailed his arms around, trying to undo the straps of his armor. His wrist gauntlets proved too heavy for him to lift. His screams filled the air as the backplate of his armor sank farther down little by little, squeezing the breath from his lungs.

"Where?" I asked again.

His bones began to break, and in what I determined to be desperation at his situation, he coughed out the words "North…sewer…room!" And then he stopped. The image burned into my eyes as his body collapsed under the pressure and his arms and legs began to swell, with the plate's weight returning to normal. He lay on the ground, eyes wide and breathless as I fell to my knees, coughing out more blood than I imagined I had.

My whole body was in pain, and my vision had blurred. I sat leaning against the shelving and book pages, trying not to succumb to the dark tunnel wrapping its way around me. Instinctively I reached out and grasped the musket. Its wood and iron rang within my grasp, leading all the pain down my arm and into the musket's rivets. I could see again, I could breathe again, and though I still felt a sting in my chest and fingers, I could almost stand. The musket itself vibrated wildly, and it took all the last of my strength to steady it until finally it calmed and all the wild air had dispersed. I would have to move quickly and across the city, no less. With weak legs I pulled myself up to my feet, stashed the papers into a satchel, and ran. With each step I swayed like an uprooting tree in a storm while my lungs burned.

I made it off the church grounds before falling to my knees and landing in a fresh puddle of rainwater. I removed my hat and tilted my head toward the black sky. The rain was cold, and every droplet was a gentle touch that eased the shakes. It was close to sunrise. Shopkeepers emerging to start their days passed by sailors leaving their families for the docks. All stopped and gawked through the oil lamplight glinting off the rain at the clipped cardinal kneeling in the street. One sailor, a young lad, stepped forward and placed his hand on my shoulder. "I know you," he said. He had already heard a story of a brave priest saving a cursed village. A priest saving a village with only the help of a Crow. A priest who let his beard grow and his hair cascade over his shoulders under a flat-brimmed, round hat. "What could bring such a man to his knees on a night so fine?" he asked. It was then a bell rang out in the distance. I grimaced at its sound, for soon would be following the footfalls of guards and the ring of swords drawn from their scabbards.

I looked at the boy. "I must get to the north-side sewer. Before he gets away." I managed to push the words, heavy as they were, to his ears. He reached down for me at the same time a clap of thunder echoed through the alleys. We turned and looked down the way behind us at the source of the percussion. A raised pistol smoked out the barrel toward the sky. Sister Mihaela stood accompanied by two guards. I had less time than I had thought. She had to have sent one guardsman or more to alert the others while she followed behind. The other guard pulled the hammer back on his pistol and took aim, telling the boy to step aside.

With one hand grasping my musket, I pulled the hammer back and told the boy to move as well. He asked me why they were after me. Briefly I told him that the church was responsible for the village and that I was trying to stop it from happening again. The guard raised his voice, telling the boy to step aside. I was still too weak or too tired to raise myself up. So the boy stepped in front of me, between me and the guard's barrel. The other guard drew his blade, and both began shouting crass vulgarities at the boy. Sister Mihaela never moved her eyes away from me.

A flurry of footsteps charging in every direction came as the reserve guards rushed down the streets to the sides of their comrades, and the boy was then backed up by other sailors and even a few of the shopkeepers. In moments the space between windows had filled with shouting guards and stout citizens standing between me and the sister. A command to disperse was shouted into the air followed by the percussion once more, then by the scream of someone I did not see. The street erupted.

Before I could pull myself to my feet, a pair of large hands wrapped themselves around me and rushed me away. I looked up to see the face of a large, burly man with stubble all across his cheeks. The courier had lifted me to my feet and was leading me away, leading me north. The sounds of the fighting grew no quieter as we traveled the north paths faster than my legs had any right to move. We soon stood above a narrow staircase nearly hidden behind an unmarked building. The door at the bottom was already propped open, and from it poured a thick, sickly yellow haze.

The rounded brick ceilings hung low, connecting walls wide apart enough for my companion and me to stand shoulder to shoulder. The ground was dry, as though the system had not been used in some time. He held his lantern forward, and we moved slowly, being careful not to make too much noise, as the air was foul and cold, sending the hairs on our necks to their ends. We ventured into the small dark for I don't know how long until we spotted a light shining ahead of us, not dim and dancing like the light of a lantern but bright and strong like that of a dozen fires. We continued our descent down the corridor until we came to the source of the light.

A large junction was lit by braziers in between the halls. The ruts in the floor had been covered with wooden planks to provide even footing. Adorning the room were a table with an additional fire underneath causing a rot-colored liquid to bubble through a series of glass tubes, a circle of upright coffins housing seven decrepit corpses, and one empty coffin. A man hunched over a small desk was scribbling into a book.

Bishop Gregory placed the pen back into its well and stood. "For ages mankind has fought back against the dark. Where a claw would reach for a babe, a stone would meet. Where two more would come, so then would bronze, then iron and the arrow and the powder. Through all the pain and loss and fear of the cold night, our mother would bring the light so long as we loved her. Then the night became calm, and we…we became complicit, greedy, unholy. The attacks on the villages drove so many into the arms of our goddess once more. They came flocking to us, to me, as lost sheep to their shepherd. Nasty, filthy pagans, unbelievers trusting in their devils and tools rather than the mother of us all. The true god, Erëdna of light, Erëdna the loving, Erëdna of a lavish desire. We could be with her, in her together, Jaccob. Help me show the filth why we once feared the dark. Why we begged Erëdna to take us into her."

I was too stunned to speak. My eyes began to water at the man who had raised me undoing himself in a manner I could not have imagined. My eyes came to the corpses in the center of the room, and all I could muster was the question "Why?"

He then spoke: "Many rejected the transformation. First they had to be starved and then fed the flesh of another human being. Working the magics of their devils proved more difficult than I had expected; however, I was able to overcome my obstacle. I found that killing the individual first and preserving the body worked just as well if not better in some cases. Some cases. There were, of course, exceptions. Some still refused the transformation even in death, those with strong attachments to the demons of the world. They had to be disposed of entirely."

My eyes traced his down one of the corridors to a faintly lit pile of mutilated bodies spawning flies and giving home to rats. My companion fell to his knees and retched the contents of his stomach to the floor. My hands shook, and the room began to spin in my eyes. I raised the barrel of my musket and shouldered the butt.

With a grimace of disappointment, Bishop Gregory said, "Come now, Jaccob. With all those books you snuck off with, this is the conclusion you reach? Perhaps I was too lenient on you. Then again, you did choose texts of ridiculous notions. I suppose I shouldn't be too surprised; my ego must have gotten the better of me. Thinking your actions in the village proved you a suitable cardinal. Clearly you survived out of luck." He stepped toward me, "I'm curious, then, as to how you will handle the transformation."

My ears felt as though they were going to bleed once the hammer struck. The chamber reverberated with the deep, heavy thunder of the musket ball launching forward in a plume of smoke and fire. It met the bishop in the chest. He tumbled backward into his desk before finally hitting the ground. He looked up at me, trying to speak through the blood filling his mouth and spilling out onto the ground. I was cold. My eyes overflowed with tears, and I felt an empty rage bouncing in and out of me, begging for a safe place to land, of which I had none to give.

I was frozen in place, watching the man who had raised me bleed to death on the floor of a sewer, when through the tears I noticed him mouthing another word. The coffin nearest me looked...wrong. The writing etched into its side began to fracture, and the corpse inside began to writhe like a snake's body without its head, twisting and turning in on itself! The blood pooled under the bishop started to dry, and he began to rise off the ground. One arm pushed him to his side and flipped him to a seated position. The bloodstain on his robe dried as well, and he could now breathe unhindered. "One shot," he said.

Before he could raise himself to his feet, I rushed forward almost against my will and raised the musket high! My hands and lungs stung. With each violent sting surging through my body, I took a deep breath, placed the pain into the wood and iron, and brought the butt down again and again and again and again onto the bishop! I heard his bones cracking with each strike and the uncanny sound of the bones setting themselves in place again until the sound of my own screams drowned out all sense. His body writhed like the corpses in their boxes, and at one point I could have sworn I saw his eyes glint in the glow of the fire like a coyote's.

I walked over to the table of chemicals and bubbling rot and pushed it over. I turned to see my companion, and before the tunnel enveloping my eyes took hold, I saw the corpses in the center had turned to ash.

I awoke some time later dazed and lacking in energy. The room was dark, but enough light shone through the bars to my side to suggest the small size of it. I very slowly and with great pain sat up and found myself on the side of a cot. A wet cloth fell from my head as I did so. The light passing through the slits between the iron changed as what looked like the silhouette of a person passed, casting their shadow across the confines.

When my eyes adjusted, I found a small table next to me with a pitcher of water and a cup.

I sat in my new dwelling wondering how I had come to be here, who had placed me in these rags, and whether or not I deserved to be here. I was not angry, nor was I scared, but instead I saw the cold walls around me as a natural consequence of what I had done. My head felt too heavy now even for my own hands. I called not for any guard or steward, for clearly there were those who knew where I was and, should they have the intention of hearing my words, would have had someone here with me to listen to them. I sat in silence and drank of the water I had been given until my head proved indeed too heavy to hold.

It was not long after I had laid my head down that more shadows began to appear on the walls. A rattling came from the opposite side of the bars before the creaking of old hinges shook my ears. I was beckoned out and was led down the hall and out to a courtyard. The sun hurt my eyes. I thought it fitting, as now they joined the rest of my body. It took me a moment to realize that I had been walked out, chained, into the center of a crowd. Two individuals stood with me. I heard murmuring rotate through the surrounding people until it came to those two that stood before me.

"Many here have branded you a witch, menace to our society, a monster. Have you anything to say on your behalf?"

I ventured my weary eyes around me. I saw no city guard, no discernible officials; instead there were simply people. Shopkeepers and mothers, children and farmers. Between me and the two seemingly speaking for or against me was a table with books and letters wrapped with blue ribbon and my own diary. I knew not what to say to these people. I don't know if I wanted to say anything or if anything should have been said at all. But the crowd waited with anticipation, and through the hard, raspy breath that filled my lungs, I spoke: "Claws and teeth do not a monster make, but their actions and the consequences that follow." I looked at the two in front of me. "I am quite tired, and I would like to lie down." One of the two nodded, and from behind me two hands placed themselves on my shoulders and walked me back to the cell. The crowd erupted behind me.

I was given a bowl with hot soup and a new pitcher of water with a candle for light. It was tomato and basil. A novelty, as I had never had that soup before and found my delight at its taste humorous given my circumstances. A knock on one of the bars broke my distraction. Entering my cell, chair in tow, was a large, burly man with bad stubble who reeked of alcohol. We both sat for a brief moment, waiting for the other to speak. He introduced himself, stating that we hadn't had the pleasure before. Rupert. Rupert Danuüt he was, and we shook hands.

Through the shakes in my body, I asked with great effort, "What happened?" And he told me everything. I had blacked out after killing Bishop Gregory, and it had been two days since. There had been fighting in the streets when Rupert had whisked me away. One of the guards shot the boy who had stood to defend me, and chaos swiftly followed. Three were killed, and fifteen were wounded. A number of the guards and a mob of citizens gave chase to Rupert and me, and they found us in the sewer. Rupert had been trying to carry me out at the time and urged them to explore farther in. He explained that the guards refused but were forced in by the mob. According to him it was a miracle we hadn't been trampled.

Rupert's eyes began to well as he spoke the next part, apologizing to me. My friends, the one I had been looking for—Mara—had all been found in the pile of discarded corpses. My heart sank, and my eyes let loose with tears. Rupert stood from his chair and sat down next to me, putting his arm around my shoulder. He continued, saying that they had found journals written in the bishop's hand cataloging each of his experiments: the names and information he had on each person that was or had been attempted to turn into the grotesque creatures let loose on the villages and the names of those he planned to test next. Many of the names were of those he seemed to consider of no consequence—people who wouldn't be missed. But as the experiments had gone on, names of those involved started to appear, including Rupert himself, the guard captain, and the duke of the city, along with "unfaithful prying eyes in the church."

"One of the guards tried to take and hide the writings and was promptly shot by another," Rupert said. "After reading through the journals and the correspondences in your satchel along with your writings, it was decided to storm the duke's palace. One of his personal men must have slipped away in the fighting to warn him. He had fled the city by the time the doors were broken down. They tore his palace apart and found letters incriminating him for his involvement as well as a plan for removal of additional parties involved should their plans begin to fall apart." Rupert said the duke had attempted to back out but was swayed by Bishop Gregory. With the new bodies rushing the church and city seeking refuge and salvation, Gregory had gained more influence over and outside of the city and had bribed the duke with an influx of copper and promises of sanctity and protection.

We again sat in silence. It was a large deal for both of us to take in, and the silence was appreciated. Composing himself, Rupert finally spoke. He had been found not guilty the day before I awoke due to "ignorance." They had yet to reach a decision on my behalf. I had been found guilty of practicing witchcraft and consorting with a pagan. This divided the newly appointed council of citizens. Some called for a burning, while others called for a more humane punishment, such as hanging by the neck, given the circumstances.

As I was faced with these possibilities, I found myself unable to blame any of them. I had spent my life believing in the impurities of those that practiced the arcane. Even if I never touched a book of spells or fastened a wand of thistle again, as long as I was in the city, there would be those that feared me. I doubted I would be able to convince anyone otherwise. Rupert then stood and said his goodbye. He was getting on a ship and leaving. Before he went I was able to thank him.

Again, I was alone in my cell. The fire of the candle dwindled as footsteps approached from the hall. Appearing in front of me was one of the two individuals that had stood with me in the crowd. A homely man with a soft smile. "It has been decided that you are allowed to leave the city but are not to return," he said with a sigh. "Your personal effects will be returned to you. You will be given a tent, imagine that, and you will leave tomorrow." I was astonished at this news, to say the least. "I suppose it is the best outcome we could give you. At least better than a hanging, at any rate," he said.

I was left in my cell until the next morning, when light trickled in. I had not slept. Each time my eyes closed, I was plagued by tremors and flashes of so many faces screaming at me in silent terror. I was perhaps all too happy when the cell door was opened and I was led through the streets to the gate of my request. I was given everything as promised. My hat and coat, sword and musket, horse, and a small amount of supplies—the tent and some bread mostly. One was kind enough to provide me with a can of coffee grounds, saying my eyes looked as though they needed it.

The walk was long. Most of the road had been washed out from the rain, and I had to lead my horse rather than sitting in the saddle. I took this time to look around me at the light passing through the branches of the trees highlighting the dust drifting by. When I would rest, I would admire the way pebbles were shaped and run my hands through the dirt just to feel the sensation. I admired and wondered at every sound coming from the brush, trying to imagine the creature making it, and ogled at every insect and bird fluttering by. I even had the novel idea of sketching one or two before deciding my skills as an artist were decisively lacking. I took my time traveling the path due to its rocks and roots and washed-away portions and out of fear.

I was scared to see the village again and see it I did. I stood outside the gates, or where they might have been, looking in. It was hollow. There was no sound to be heard save the chirp of the occasional bird in the trees. No one deconstructing the mess of rope and wood and nails lining the roofs, no fires to rest at, and no children to spread cheer. It was simply hollow. The ground had caved in, swallowing the village whole. All that remained was dust and water and a single cresting portion of a roof. I stood for some time watching the ripples dwindle at the reach of the shore until they stopped altogether.

A chill ran down my spine, and an odd reflection of the water turned my eye upward. Suspended above the water was the body of a woman hanging from the neck, swaying in a breeze that could not be felt. Her eyes bulged from her skull. She spoke not, nor did she moan any ghastly wails or twitch and pull at the rope. She hung still, staring at me and swaying in a breeze. "We both chose our paths, didn't we?" My voice was surprisingly callous in my ears.

In the blink of an eye, the hanging woman disappeared, and the shore collected its ripples again. I took one last look at the hollowed, mutilated ruins of the village before walking to the opposite end of the lake. On this end, stuck into the dirt was a large stick with a plank of wood tied to it, and carved into the plank were the words, "Myers, we made it." My heart near leaped out of my chest, and so I headed into the forest.

The paths became more of a suggestion the farther into the trees I walked. What simple wonders I found around me in the bark of a tree and the veins of the leaves and so on until I eventually came to rest. The sky was darkening as I set my tent to the ground and roused a small fire. I looked toward each snap of a branch with a hint of fear and an odd hope to see a pair of glinting eyes looking back at me. As the night grew, my mind wondered what would become of the ghoul. Would it stay safe in the forest?

My thoughts were interrupted when a pair of dirty boots emerged from the darkness, stopping across my fire from me. I looked up to see a man, disheveled and brandishing a knife. "Well, hello, my friend," I said.

The man's face was a cross between a sneer and a smug grin of self-importance. "All right then, friend, let's have it," he said.

I answered, "Of course, you need only have a seat." I pointed to the ground next to me.

The man seemed amused at my gesture. "You're telling me that if I have a seat, you'll give me what you have?" He laughed.

"Not all of it, but yes," I replied.

His amusement quickly faded, and while I was sure his sentence was going to be longer when he said, "Looks like you only have enough for one," I interrupted him by saying, "And yet I'm willing to share." I then offered him the coffee I had brewed over the fire. After a sniffle from his nose, he drew the blade back into his belt and sat down next to me. We sat silently for long stretches of time—I think because neither of us knew what to say to the other. I really didn't mind the silence. I allowed my thoughts to wander once more until eventually he fell asleep, and my nightmares kept me awake.

When morning came and my eyes opened from a nearly sleepless night, I found the man walking out of the woods once more toward me carrying a pair of rabbits over his shoulder. He sat down again and started to prepare them, looking at me once in a while. I relit the fire and put on the last of the coffee.

We traveled together through the day until the trees stopped and opened into a great valley with brooks and streams running through it, encircled by rolling, tree-covered mountains. He proved to be pleasant company and spoke of his many travels. He had once been a fur trader before a fire struck the forest he frequented and was forced to scrape and claw for bread and meat. He then asked me where I was going as we stood on the edge of the forest. "To see a friend," I said.

"Might I come with you?" he asked. I pondered his question for a moment.

"I would like that," I replied. "I would like that."

CPSIA information can be obtained
at www.ICGtesting.com
Printed in the USA
BVHW030316100123
655977BV00012B/125